MW01096458

HER BILLIONAIRE EX-BOYFRIEND FAKE FIANCÉ

CHRISTMAS IN EMERALD FALLS

CHRISTINE KERSEY

SAPPHIRE CREEK PRESS

The characters and events portrayed in this book are fictitious. Any similarity to real persons, living or dead, is coincidental and not intended by the author.

Her Billionaire Ex-Boyfriend Fake Fiancé

Copyright © 2019 by Christine Kersey

All rights reserved

No part of this book may be reproduced, or stored in a retrieval system, or transmitted in any form or by any means, electronic, mechanical, photocopying, recording, or otherwise, without express written permission of the publisher.

❀ Created with Vellum

BOOKS BY CHRISTINE KERSEY

Emerald Falls Romance Series

Crushing On You (Emerald Falls, Book One)

Dangerous Lies (Emerald Falls, Book Two)

Chance Encounter (Emerald Falls, Book Three)

Her Billionaire Ex-Boyfriend Fake Fiancé (Christmas in Emerald Falls)

Fair Catch Romance

Protected by the Quarterback

False Start

Blindsided

Pass Interference

Pass Protection

Game On

Pandemic

Pandemic: The Beginning (Pandemic Book One)

Forced Exodus (Pandemic Book Two)

No Safe Place (Pandemic Book Three)

Ashley's Billionaire

Snowed in with the Billionaire

Assistant to the Billionaire

Trouble with the Billionaire

Ever After with the Billionaire

Billionaires Find Love

The Protective Billionaire

The Missing Billionaire

Park City Firefighter Romance

Rescue My Heart

Hearts On Fire

Searching for Love

Falling for You (Searching for Love, Book One)

Finding Reese (Searching for Love, Book Two)

Surrender My Heart (Searching for Love, Book Three)

Bring Me Home (Searching for Love, Book Four)

Lily's Story

He Loves Me Not (Lily's Story, Book 1)

Don't Look Back (Lily's Story, Book 2)

Love At Last (Lily's Story, Book 3)

Life Imperfect (Lily's Story, Book 4)

Parallel World

Dare to Resist (Parallel World Book One)

Dare to Endure (Parallel World Book Two)

Dare to Defy (Parallel World Book Three)

Dare to Oppose (Parallel World Book Four)

Dare to Prevail (Parallel World Book Five)

Over You Series

Over You

Second Chances (sequel to Over You)

Witness Series

Witness (Witness, Book 1)

Retribution (Witness, Book 2)

Standalone Suspense

Suspicions

No Way Out

CHAPTER 1

"Who does he think he is?" Ashleigh Hopkins glared at the screen of her phone as she sat on her couch, the picture of Chase Matthews taunting her.

"Who are you talking about?" her sister Melanie asked as she walked into the living room. It was Ashleigh's house, but her sister and four-year-old niece lived there with her.

Embarrassed that her sister had caught her noticing anything about Chase Matthews, Ashleigh felt her face heat. "No one."

Melanie sprang forward and snatched the phone from Ashleigh's hand. "You don't get away with it that easily, Ash. I want to know who's getting under your skin." Melanie looked at the screen, her eyebrows shooting up, then her eyes shifted to Ashleigh.

Embarrassed for her sister to find out that she ever

thought about Chase, Ashleigh let her emotions rule her voice. "Give that back to me."

Tilting her head, Melanie asked, "Since when do you follow Chase Matthews on social media?"

Sighing heavily, but only because she couldn't come up with a good excuse as to why she was looking at pictures of her ex-boyfriend, Ashleigh stood and held out her hand. "That's none of your business."

Melanie murmured, "Uh-huh," but at least she gave the phone back.

Tucking the phone in her back pocket, Ashleigh asked, "Isn't it time for you to go to work?"

Melanie chuckled. "Not yet."

Just then, an adorable little girl came bounding in the room, flinging herself at Melanie. "Mommy!"

Melanie swung her up in a hug. "Hi, Avery."

Glad her sister was distracted, Ashleigh took the opportunity to go into the kitchen and take another peek at the picture Chase had posted. In it, he was dressed in a tuxedo and had not one, but two gorgeous women with him—one on each arm.

As she stared at the picture, she remembered when she had been the one on his arm. His one and only, he used to say. Well, that certainly wasn't the case any longer. Sure, it had been six years since she'd last seen him—in person, that is. But it still hurt when she saw him with another girl.

"What are you doing?" Melanie said from right behind her.

Ashleigh let out a yelp as she jerked away from her annoying older sister and spun around to glare at her.

Melanie chuckled. "I thought you were over him."

"I *am* over him. Totally over him." She hoped she'd convinced Melanie, because someone needed to believe it.

"Right."

"I am. Now, I *do* have to go to work, so if you'll excuse me."

"Of course." Sweeping her hand out to the side, Melanie stepped back.

Frowning, Ashleigh walked past her, grabbed her purse from the kitchen counter, and walked out the front door.

On the way to the Emerald Falls Library where she worked as the librarian, Ashleigh struggled to push aside the image of Chase galavanting with those women. Of course, she didn't know if he was *actually* galavanting. For all she knew, once the camera was turned off he'd sent them both on their way, that they meant nothing to him.

Just like she meant nothing to him.

Shoving down the memory of their last conversation, when he'd shattered her heart and left Emerald Falls, she focused on driving.

She pulled into a parking space, tossed her purse over her shoulder, and climbed out of her car. As she unlocked the single glass door and walked inside the library, the absolute quiet immediately soothed her, and the familiar scent of rows and rows of lovely books sent a blanket of calm wrapping around her. She loved the library—always had. Ten years earlier, when she'd turned sixteen and had gotten her driver's license, the first place she'd driven on her own was the library. Browsing aisle after aisle of books without worrying about having to call someone for a ride had been an unknown luxury up until that point. Now though, it had become routine.

She went to her desk, which was in the front of the library where patrons could easily find her to get help, and booted up her computer.

The glass door opened and a woman about the same age as Ashleigh walked in. Ashleigh smiled at her. "Hey, Taylor."

Taylor strode over to Ashleigh's desk and set down a stack of books with a frown. "Hey."

"What's wrong?" Wait. Did she really want to know? Inevitably it had to do with Taylor's boyfriend, Seth.

"Seth—"

Ashleigh threw her hand up. "Let me stop you there."

Taylor's eyebrows shot up and her mouth fell open. "What?"

After seeing the pictures of Chase, she just wasn't in the mood to hear about someone else's boyfriend problems—not that there was a chance Chase would ever be her boyfriend again. Even hinting at that thought brought a rush of heat to her face.

"If you don't want to know what's wrong," Taylor said with a frown, "then don't ask."

This was *Taylor's* boyfriend they were talking about. Not Ashleigh's ex. She sighed. "I'm sorry. What happened?"

Taylor grabbed a chair, dragged it over to Ashleigh's desk, and plopped into it. "Well…"

Oh boy. This was going to take a while. Bracing herself, Ashleigh relaxed her shoulders and gave her full attention to Taylor.

"On Saturday Seth was supposed to take me dancing, but at the last minute he said his friend got tickets to the Sacramento Kings game. Well, you know Seth. He can't pass up an opportunity to watch the NBA. So, he dropped me and our date like a bad habit."

Ashleigh nodded. So typical. "See? This is exactly why I'm on a man-fast."

Taylor burst out laughing. "A what?"

Was it really such a ridiculous idea? "A man-fast. You know, staying away from all men."

"Oh. I can figure out what it means. I just don't know why you would want to be on one."

Really? Did she have to explain? "Every man I've dated has turned into a flake. We go out once or twice, and then poof, it's like he was a figment of my imagination."

Taylor shook her head. "You just haven't found the right man yet."

"You're saying you have?"

"Well, I love Seth and he loves me. It's just, sometimes, you know, he forgets that he wants to be with me every minute."

Chuckling, Ashleigh shook her head.

Taylor smirked. "I'll get you on a date one way or another."

Ashleigh rolled her eyes. "There's a big stack of books that came in over the weekend that needs checking in.

"All right, all right." Taylor stood. "We're putting up the Christmas decorations today, aren't we?"

With the distraction of seeing the picture of Chase, Ashleigh had completely forgotten about that. She adored Christmas and had been looking forward all weekend to decorating the library. She'd made herself wait until the beginning of December. Now, the wait was over. "That's right."

"Yay!"

Just what she needed to forget about Chase Matthews.

CHAPTER 2

$\mathcal{C}$hase Matthews was deeply concerned. In his office, he was on the phone with his sister, Jordyn. She'd called to let him know that their mom was sick. Like, seriously sick.

"You need to come to home," she said.

Even though Emerald Falls, where he'd grown up, was about a ninety-minute drive from where he lived in Cupertino, California, Chase hadn't been there in months. He'd been too busy growing his cybersecurity firm. And business was booming. In his wildest dreams he'd never thought he'd be so successful.

"Can you come?" Jordyn pressed. "I mean, it's almost Christmas. You were going to come home for Christmas, weren't you?"

Truth was, he hadn't planned on it. Hadn't really thought

that far ahead. But this was his mom. When his father had left them when he was eight years old, he'd been crushed. But his mom had picked up the pieces and had helped them go on. He would do anything for her. Already had, as a matter of fact. Paying off her mortgage and making sure she didn't have to work if she didn't want to. But this illness? It was a new wrinkle in her life—in all of their lives.

"Is it cancer?" he asked, dreading the answer. "Is it back?"

Jordyn was silent, which answered his question in the most devastating way. "They think it's spread," she said, her voice soft. "I think...I think we might need to consider hospice care soon."

How had it gotten so bad so fast without him knowing? It had been three years since his mom had battled breast cancer. He'd thought it was in her past. Had he been purposefully ignorant of reality? Too focused on his business to think about his family? He didn't know. All he knew was that he needed to go home to Emerald Falls. "Yeah," he said without hesitation, "I need to wrap up a few things here, but I'll drive out there later today."

"Thank you, Chase."

"I'll see you soon."

He disconnected the call, leaned back in his chair, and sighed deeply. If he were to lose his mom, he didn't know what he would do. He would effectively be an orphan. It was true that as far as he knew his father was still alive, but when his father had left them, he'd never looked back and Chase had no idea where he was. He could afford to hire someone to track him down, but why would he? Clearly, the man had no desire to be in touch with his children. It had been twenty years since his father had left, but even now, the memory of him just not being there any longer still hurt.

Anyway, it wasn't about Chase and how he felt. His mom was sick. He needed to do whatever he could to alleviate her suffering. And to just spend time with her.

CHAPTER 3

*E*arly that evening, as Chase drove into Emerald Falls and saw Christmas lights twinkling in the trees that lined Main Street, a calmness settled over him and memories from when he lived there filled his mind. As he passed restaurants, diners, and other places he used to hang out, he thought about his friends, but one face kept filling his mind. Ashleigh Hopkins. Her sparkling smile and long blonde hair, her blue eyes and bubbly personality. She'd been with him at all of those places in town. They'd dated for a year, but then he'd graduated from college and his ambition had taken over. He'd left Emerald Falls to pursue his dream of running his own business without a backward glance.

That had been six years before. Now, he was his own boss, had more money than he knew what to do with, and could—and did—date any woman he wanted.

Then why did Ashleigh's face stubbornly refuse to leave his mind?

Didn't matter. He was there to see his mom and his sister. That was it. Besides, he doubted he'd run in to Ashleigh. She was probably married with a passel of kids by now. Maybe he'd ask Jordyn. Scratch that. He didn't want his sister to know Ashleigh had crossed his mind.

He turned down his mom's street and pulled into her driveway. Lights from a Christmas tree winked in the front window—thanks to Jordyn, he was sure. He was grateful for his younger sister. She'd chosen to stay in Emerald Falls after college. Still single, she was a promising artist, building her portfolio while living at home and helping their mom.

Chase strode up the walkway. The front door burst open before he reached it.

"Chase!" Jordyn said, her bright smile filling Chase with warmth. She dashed toward him and threw her arms around him.

He held her, relishing the affection of his only sibling. They'd been close growing up, and though he hadn't seen her in months, it felt like no time had passed at all.

He pulled away and appraised her. Tall and slender with long auburn hair and delicate features, Jordyn had turned into a gorgeous woman.

He smiled at her. "Hey, sis." His smile slid off of his face. "How's Mom?"

Jordyn took him by the hand and led him inside. "Excited to see *you*."

They walked inside, the heat from the fireplace warming the living room. Chase's mom slowly stood as he entered the room.

She was thinner than he remembered, and the way she moved told him she was uncomfortable.

"Mom." He drew her into a gentle embrace, the thought of losing her suddenly overwhelming him. Inhaling deeply to get control of his emotions, Chase released her and smiled at her. "It's so good to see you."

"Thank you for coming," she said, her smile as bright as ever.

Guilt that he hadn't come sooner, and that he'd needed something so serious to get him there, washed over him. But he was there now. That's what mattered. And he would stay as long she needed him.

"Sit," she said, bringing him to the couch where she sat beside him. "Tell me what's new."

They spoke on the phone from time to time, so she knew all about his business. Chase knew what she was really asking—how was his love life? "Nothing new to report."

"No one serious, then?"

"Nope."

"Well," she said with raised eyebrows, "I'm glad you're not actually interested in those women I keep seeing in social media pictures."

Chase glanced at Jordyn, whose lips were compressed like she was trying to suppress a laugh. He turned back to his mom. "Why not? What's wrong with them?"

"Wearing those skimpy dresses and hanging all over you? Come on, Chase. That's not the type of woman I want to be the mother of my grandchildren."

Having children was the *last* thing on his mind, but he wasn't about to argue with her. Not when he'd just gotten there. Not when she was so ill. "Duly noted."

She sighed. "I don't think you're taking this seriously."

Here we go. "I know you wish I was married and had kids, but first I have to find the right woman."

Tears filled her eyes, which dug deep into Chase's heart. "Mom, please don't cry."

She rested her head on his shoulder. "It's just...I'm so scared that I won't live to see you get your happily ever after."

He put his arm around her as a knot clogged his throat. The thought of her not being around long enough to witness him getting married tore at his insides. It wasn't that he was in a hurry to get married, but the truth was, he wouldn't *mind* if he found the right woman. Everything else in his life was going so well, it actually felt like the right time to finally start looking for someone to spend the rest of his life with. But would it happen while his mom was still around to witness it?

CHAPTER 4

"*B*y the way," Taylor said to Ashleigh as they strung tinsel in the children's section, "how is the fundraising going?"

Ashleigh frowned. She'd been trying to raise money to purchase more computers, books, and audiobooks for the library—something the town of Emerald Falls should have paid for but didn't have the funds for. So, she'd taken it upon herself to raise the money. Their little library only had two computers for all of their patrons to use—not nearly enough. She wanted to buy six more, plus the library hadn't been able to buy enough copies of books and audiobooks to satisfy demand. Lately, raising money for the library had become her passion project. She'd gotten a few small businesses to donate some money and she'd organized a fundraiser, which would be held that Friday.

"So far, I've raised enough to buy two additional computers," she said.

"That's great!"

"Yes, but we need so much more." She was thrilled with
her progress, but there was a long way to go. It was overwhelming.

"You'll do it, Ash. I know you will."

She appreciated Taylor's confidence, and as she handed
Taylor another string of silver tinsel, she said, "I have high
hopes for the auction at the fundraiser."

"I'm sure we'll raise a lot of money with the goods that
our local businesses donated."

Ashleigh was so grateful for the help the community was
giving.

Taylor taped a section of tinsel to the ceiling. "Who's on
board for sure?"

Ashleigh pictured the faces of her friends who owned
businesses. "Gage is donating baked goods from his Sprinkles of Joy bakery, and Amethyst said she would bring
several pieces from her jewelry collection." She listed off
several other people who had committed to donating items.
"Clarissa from Eats & Treats is catering." And the Emerald
Falls Hotel had donated their ballroom for the event. Just
thinking about the whole thing excited her. It would be a
fabulous night.

Taylor nodded, then her face lit up. "Oh! I almost forgot
to tell you the good news. I got Jordyn Matthews. She's going

to donate one of her paintings. Have you seen her work? It's amazing."

The mention of Chase's younger sister sent a jolt through Ashleigh. During the year Ashleigh and Chase had dated, Ashleigh had eaten dinner with him and his mom and sister a number of times. Even so, Jordyn had been a teenager. She'd been busy with her own life and she and Ashleigh had never gotten close. And after Chase had left her, Ashleigh hadn't seen much of his family.

But Jordyn was Chase's sister. Then again, what difference did that make? Chase was off doing his thing. It's not like being around Jordyn was the same thing as being around Chase. Besides, Ashleigh would do pretty much anything to raise money for her passion project. "Oh. That's great." Her tone was less than enthusiastic.

"Why are you acting weird?"

That's right. Taylor had no idea of Ashleigh's history with Chase. Plastering a smile onto her lips, Ashleigh said, "Weird? What are you talking about?" Before Taylor could reply, Ashleigh turned around and said, "Looks like that person needs help." Then she hurried away.

CHAPTER 5

efore Ashleigh knew it, it was Friday night, and as she looked over everything at the venue, she got nervous that something would go wrong. "What am I forgetting?" she murmured as her gaze sweep over the beautifully set tables.

"Stop worrying," Taylor said as she materialized beside her. "Everything's going to be perfect." Then she grinned like there was something she was keeping to herself.

Ashleigh narrowed her eyes. "What?"

A little giggle escaped Taylor's lips. "It's nothing."

Placing a hand on her hip, Ashleigh tilted her head. "You're making me nervous."

"I promise. It's all good."

Having no choice but to trust her friend, Ashleigh pushed down her concerns. Instead, she focused on the auction items that were being set out by the donors. Needing a distraction, Ashleigh made a beeline to Amethyst, who was laying out the handmade jewelry she was donating.

"Everything is gorgeous, Amethyst. Thank you so much for donating these."

Amethyst, her red hair gleaming, turned to Ashley and gave her a quick hug. "I'm glad to help, Ash. This is such a great cause."

After chatting with Amethyst, she went to say hello to Melanie, who was helping Gage set out his baked goods.

"Hey, you two."

Melanie set down a plate of beautifully decorated cupcakes, then gave Ashleigh a hug. "How's it going?"

"So far so good." She smiled at Gage. "Thank you for doing this, Gage."

He returned her smile, his gray eyes sparkling. "You should be thanking Melanie. If it wasn't for her, I don't know if I would have donated nearly this much." He put an arm around Melanie, who gazed at him with obvious love.

It warmed Ashleigh's heart to see her sister so content. She'd been through some rough times in her life and she deserved this happiness.

A few moments later, guests started arriving. "Excuse me," she said to Gage and Melanie before hurrying over to greet the people coming through the door. Each guest had paid to come and every dollar would go to the library, so Ashleigh wanted to make sure each person knew how much she appreciated them.

Before long, everyone was seated. Almost every seat was filled, which pleased Ashleigh tremendously. There was an empty seat here and there, but Ashleigh was beyond grateful for the people in her community. She picked up the microphone and greeted everyone, thanking them for their support.

"After dinner we'll be auctioning off a number of items." She swept her hand toward the items on display, then she faced the crowd again. "Until then, enjoy your meal."

CHAPTER 6

*C*hase was running late. He was supposed to go to some fundraiser that Jordyn was involved in. He didn't know much about it, just that the library was raising money. Seemed like a good cause, and since Jordyn and their mom had invited him to come, he'd agreed. He'd just had a meeting to finish first. Oh well. Better late than never.

He parked his black Lamborghini Aventador and headed inside the hotel where the event was taking place. The room was crowded, but it didn't take long to find Jordyn and their mom—even though she wasn't feeling great, she'd insisted on coming to support the library.

Chase strode to their table and took the empty seat they'd saved, which was right between them.

"Glad you could make it," Jordyn said with a smirk, then she continued eating her salad.

Smiling, he shook his head. Moments later a server brought him a salad. "Thank you," he said to the girl. He turned to his sister. "Good turnout."

Focused on her salad, she nodded. "Yeah. I'm sure Ashleigh's thrilled."

Wait, what? His eyebrows shot up. Surely his sister didn't mean Ashleigh Hopkins. Emerald Falls was a small town, but the name Ashleigh wasn't that uncommon, was it?

Then he saw her in full and living color. Standing near the front talking to another woman. It had been six years since he'd broken up with her and bolted, but she looked exactly the same—poised and polished and... well, stunning. He couldn't tear his eyes away from her.

"How was your meeting?" his mom asked.

Dragging his gaze away from Ashleigh and to his mom, Chase said, "It was good." Who cared about his meeting when his old flame was standing across the room and had no idea he was there? What would she do when she saw him? Throw one of the pies on the display table at him? Most likely. After all, he'd left without a second look and had never even reached out to her. From her point of view, he was a selfish jerk.

"What's wrong?" Jordyn asked him, evidently unaware of the turmoil going on inside him. She glanced at his untouched salad. "Aren't you hungry?"

Actually, he was starving, but he couldn't think about food just then. Not when a million questions raced through his mind. "What does Ashleigh have to do with this fundraiser?"

Jordyn made a face that said *duh, how do you not know this?* "Only everything."

Annoyed with his sister for treating him like an imbecile, he scowled. "In case you've forgotten, I no longer live here. So, please, fill me in."

Jordyn dipped her chin. "Sorry." She smiled. "Ashleigh's the librarian and she's raising money for computers and books and stuff for Emerald Falls' library. I donated one of my paintings for the auction."

There was an auction? He would buy something. For a lot of money. Maybe that would help Ashleigh not hate him. Better yet, he'd write a big check. But would she accept it? He'd find a way to make her. He could even do it anonymously. Yeah, that would work. Wait. Then it wouldn't help her not hate him.

Not sure what he would do, but wanting to do something big, he smiled at Jordyn. "Okay. Thanks."

"You're welcome."

He picked up his fork and began eating his salad, all the while acutely aware of Ashleigh and her every move.

Everything was going perfectly. People looked happy, the food was delicious, everyone who'd promised something for the auction had come through. The night couldn't be going any better.

"Come sit down," Taylor said to Ashleigh, practically dragging her to their table.

She had no appetite—stress did that to her—but she moved the food on her plate around and took a bite from time to time while making conversation with the people at her table.

When dessert was served, Ashleigh turned to Taylor. "Time to start the auction."

Taylor's face lit up. "Yay! This is going to be so fun."

"You'll be a great auctioneer." Taylor had volunteered the moment Ashleigh had told her about the fundraiser.

Taylor pushed her chair back. "Thanks." Then she grinned in that way she had earlier, like she had a secret. Ashleigh narrowed her eyes. What was going on? Before she could ask, Taylor scurried to the front of the room and picked up the microphone.

"Hello, hello, hello! I hope everyone enjoyed their meal."

Heads nodded as others voiced their pleasure.

"The Emerald Falls Library wants to thank Clarissa from Eats & Treats for donating all the food for tonight's fundraiser. We also want to thank everyone who donated items for our auction. We couldn't have done this without you."

Ashleigh applauded with everyone else, so appreciative of her community.

With a bright smile, Taylor said, "Now, let's start the auction!"

More applause.

Taylor began auctioning off the items, and as the bids came in, Ashleigh was thrilled. That night's fundraiser would help tremendously with buying the computers and books that she so deeply desired for the library.

All the items had been auctioned off, but then Taylor said, "We have one last item that is kind of a surprise!"

Ashleigh's eyebrows shot up. Was this the secret Taylor had been keeping? Super curious what it was, Ashleigh gave her full attention to Taylor. Taylor looked right at her, and with a tiny smirk, said, "We thought it would be fun to auction off a dinner date with our own librarian, Ashleigh Hopkins!"

What??!! Who was this *we* Taylor was talking about? When had she come up with this crazy idea? Why hadn't she warned her?

Ashleigh was about to leap to her feet and shout that this was all a joke, but then she realized all eyes were focused on her as people were clapping and smiling and nodding like they thought it was a fantastic idea. Heat blasted up her face. She would have to kill Taylor later.

"This project is so very important to Ashleigh," Taylor went on, staring right at Ashleigh like she was telling her not to make a scene, then her gaze swept the crowd. "I know whoever has the winning bid will be generous with their giving." Taylor looked right at Ashleigh again. "Let me remind you that every dollar raised will go to buying books and computers for our very own library."

Okay, she got the message. If having dinner with someone would help the library, then fine, she would do it. What was the worst that could happen?

"Let's start the bidding at five hundred dollars," Taylor said with a wide grin.

Ashleigh's eyes widened. Five hundred dollars? No one was going to pay that, and when no one did, Ashleigh would just be embarrassed by the whole thing.

The room stayed silent—so different than it had been during the rest of the auction. Mortified that no one thought she was worth that much, Ashleigh felt tears spring to her eyes. It reminded her of Chase's parting words that there was nothing for him in Emerald Falls. Which had included her.

Trying not to wallow in self-pity, Ashleigh softly cleared her throat while staring at the crumbs on her dessert plate.

"Five thousand dollars," a man's voice called out.

CHAPTER 7

G asps and a sudden rush of voices could be heard as everyone reacted to the outrageous bid.

Ashleigh was more shocked than anyone. Who had bid such an exorbitant amount? With so many people there, she couldn't see who it was. Heads were in the way as everyone else searched for the bidder. Coming halfway out of her seat, Ashleigh scanned the room.

Then she saw him.

Chase Matthews.

Her heart stopped beating and fell into her stomach. Then it went into a sprint as it tried to vault out of her chest.

What was *he* doing there? And what in the world was he doing bidding on a date with her?

"We have five thousand dollars," Taylor said, her voice incredulous.

Ashleigh couldn't see her friend's expression because her own gaze was locked on Chase, who seemed to be avoiding looking at her. In fact, his eyes had gone kind of wide, like he was just realizing what he'd done. Like he knew he'd made a mistake.

Swallowing the mixture of shock, annoyance, and anger, Ashleigh decided then and there that she would tell him he didn't have to go through with it. Well, she would make him pay the money he'd bid—she was fairly certain he could afford to. But she would tell him the date was unnecessary. In fact, she didn't want it.

She sat in her seat and turned her back on him, facing the front.

"Do we have six thousand?" Taylor asked the crowd, although from the look on her face it was obvious that she knew as well as everyone else in the room that no one was going to outbid Chase Matthews.

What had he just done? Chase wondered if he'd lost his mind. Apparently he had, but there was nothing he could do about it now.

All eyes were on him, but the only pair that mattered were Ashleigh's and she'd turned away.

He'd wanted to donate money to Ashleigh's cause so she wouldn't hate him, but forcing her to go on a date with him? Why put them both in an awkward situation? What had he been thinking? Obviously, he hadn't been.

"Sold!" Taylor said. "To the man in the back." She paused. "That concludes our auction. Thank you, everyone, for participating and for your generous donations."

Much to Chase's relief, only a few eyes lingered on him, but eventually even those turned away, although in his peripheral vision he could tell his mom and sister were staring at him. He turned to Jordyn first.

Her eyebrows were raised. "What do you think you're doing?"

"What do you mean?"

"Are you trying to show off?"

That's what she was worried about? Not that he was forcing his ex-girlfriend to go out with him when she most certainly hated him?

"No," he said. "I just, I wanted to donate to the library."

"I think it's exciting," his mom said from his other side.

He swiveled in his chair to look at her. Surely she remembered how he'd dumped Ashleigh six years earlier even if Jordyn had either forgotten or didn't care. "Exciting?"

Her gaze softened. "And romantic."

"Romantic?" He hadn't meant for his voice to go up an octave, but the idea was ludicrous.

"Yes," she said, her smile serene. "I know you still care about Ashleigh Hopkins."

"I don't know, Mom," Jordyn said, drawing Chase's attention back to her.

"Why do you say that?" their mom asked her.

31

Why did they have to discuss his failed love life in front of him? Still, he was curious to hear what Jordyn had to say.

"It's been, like, six years. I think they've both moved on."

"Right," he said, forcing out a chuckle. Then he looked in the direction he'd last seen Ashleigh, but she was nowhere to be found. Had she bolted already? But no, she wouldn't do that. This was her fundraiser. Probably off in the wings somewhere taking care of things. Either that or plotting how to destroy him.

He felt someone standing behind him. He craned his neck around and looked up to see Ashleigh standing over him wearing a pinched smile. Having her so close took his breath away—a completely unexpected reaction.

"Hi," he said dumbly.

Her eyes narrowed ever so briefly, then she turned her attention to his mom and Jordyn, giving them both a warm smile. "It's so good to see you both. Thank you for coming. And, Jordyn, thank you so much for donating that beautiful painting."

"I was happy to," Jordyn said.

As Ashleigh proceeded to chat with his mom and Jordyn, Chase felt invisible. Something he wasn't used to. And if he was honest with himself, it bothered him to have Ashleigh right there and not have her acknowledge him. Well, she'd given him that frosty look, but that hardly counted.

Unexpectedly, her attention shifted to him, and in a tone that brooked no argument, she said, "Can I talk to you?"

Chase was on his feet before his brain had a chance to

command his legs to move. It was so abrupt, in fact, that he nearly bowled Ashleigh over. She stepped back with a gasp.

Whoa. Ashleigh didn't remember Chase being so tall and muscular. Had he grown in the last six years? He'd been twenty-two the last time she'd seen him in person. Did men grow after twenty-two? Obviously he'd been working out. How else to account for the way his biceps strained against the fabric of his shirt?

"Where do you want to go?" he asked, startling her out of her appraisal of his amazing good looks.

Tearing her gaze way, she glanced over her shoulder to a corner of the ballroom before turning back and meeting his green eyes—eyes which brought back all kinds of memories. Some good and some heartbreaking, but every one of them starring Chase Matthews.

She pointed to the corner. "Over there."

She barely waited for him to nod before she turned and strode to the empty corner, dredging up all of the hurt and anger she'd felt when he'd dumped her and left town. She needed those feelings now to be able to tell him that this dinner date was *not* going to happen.

"Look," he said before she had a chance to speak, which was good since she had no idea what to say. He smiled the devastatingly handsome smile she remembered so well.

"Let's not do this, okay? I mean, I'll pay the money I bid, but we don't need to go out."

What? He was blowing *her* off? Uh-uh. Wasn't going to happen. "You paid for a date with me," she heard herself say, not believing the words that were spilling out of her mouth, "and you'll follow through. You're not going to cut and run like you did before."

Had she really just said that? What was *wrong* with her? Clearly she'd lost her mind—and all of her self-respect.

Chase recoiled, his eyes wide. "Okay."

"Good." Could she just *stop* now? She held out her hand. "Let me have your phone."

He handed it over without question.

It was as if an alien had taken over her body, but she pressed on, pulling up his messaging app and texting herself before handing his phone back. "Now you have my number. Call or text so we can get this over with." Without another word, she spun on her heel and stalked away, her mind screaming at her to go back and cancel the date, but her body refusing to cooperate.

CHAPTER 8

*C*hase watched Ashleigh sashay away, his mind reeling. What had just happened? He'd been certain she was going to spit in his face, although he hadn't known if that would be before or after she told him to get lost. Instead, she'd insisted he take her out on the date he'd bid for. Even after he'd given her a way out. One that included her keeping the five grand.

Confused, he stared at the door where Ashleigh had exited.

"That was smooth," Jordyn said from beside him.

How much had she overheard?

As if she could read his mind, she smirked and said, "All of it." Then she tilted her head. "I like that girl."

He kind of did too. Six years earlier he'd really liked her too, although he'd moved on since then, not thinking about her much at all. She'd changed though. He didn't remember her being so confident and assertive.

He liked it.

"When are you going to call her?" Jordyn asked.

"Soon." He didn't need his kid sister harassing him about this, although he knew she would.

She cocked an eyebrow. "Don't wait too long or you might lose your chance."

Was that true? Of course it was. Ashleigh was a stunningly beautiful, confident, and intelligent woman. Men had to be lining up for her. That was probably why they'd auctioned off a date with her in the first place. Too many men wanted to go out with her. And he'd won. All of a sudden he realized how serendipitous it had been that he'd attended this fundraiser. What if his meeting had kept him from coming? Some other lucky man would have won the bid and Chase wouldn't have even realized what he'd missed out on.

Yeah, he'd better get on it before he lost his chance.

"Right," he said to Jordyn, then he strode out of the ballroom and to his car.

"Are you still mad at me?" Taylor asked Ashleigh as they walked out to their cars after all the guests had left and there was nothing else for them to take care of.

Ashleigh turned and glared. "It would have been nice if you'd given me a head's up."

Taylor burst out laughing. "If I'd done that, you wouldn't have allowed me to auction off a date with you."

"Exactly," she said with exaggerated flair, her arms sweeping outward.

"But the guy who won…" Taylor's words trailed off as her eyebrows wiggled. "You gotta admit, he's hot."

That was certainly true. The memory of standing so close to him filled her mind and her face flushed. Good thing it was too dark for Taylor to see. Then she thought about the way she'd *insisted* that he take her out. What an idiot she'd been. Especially after he'd basically admitted to making a mistake in bidding on the date. Now she would have to sit with him for a couple of hours feeling like a fool, like a pity date, really.

"You're not saying anything," Taylor pointed out. "You think he's hot, right?"

Ashleigh stopped in her tracks and turned to Taylor, who stopped beside her. "I think he's an arrogant jerk." Her voice might have held a tinge of venom.

Taylor took a step back. "Whoa. What did the guy ever do to you?"

Should she enlighten her and tell her that Chase was her ex-boyfriend? That he'd flat-out told her that she wasn't worth staying for and then left town and never looked back? Mmm. Not yet. Instead, she sighed. "I'm tired."

Taylor shook her head. "Okay." She paused a beat. "That money he donated sure helped though, right?"

Couldn't Taylor let the whole thing with Chase go? Still, it was true. The five thousand dollars he'd donated was more than all of the rest of the bids combined. "Yeah."

They reached their cars.

"I'll see you later," Taylor said.

Ashleigh threw her a weary smile. "Good night. And thank you for all your help."

Taylor smirked, which Ashleigh ignored, and they both got in their cars before Ashleigh headed home. Only problem was, Melanie would be there to greet her. She'd witnessed Chase bidding on the date and Melanie knew all about Ashleigh's history with him.

Hoping to sneak in without Melanie noticing—she'd managed to avoid her at the fundraiser after Chase's winning bid—when Ashleigh got home she quietly turned the doorknob and pushed the door open.

"There you are," Melanie said with an exasperated sigh as she rushed toward her. "I'm *dying* right now. *Dying*."

That made two of them.

Melanie took her by the hand and practically dragged Ashleigh to the couch where they both sat down. "Did you know he was going to be there? I saw you talking to him afterwards. What did he say?"

Needing a moment to gather her thoughts, Ashleigh bit her lip and stared at her big sister.

"Come on. I've been waiting to talk to you since the moment Chase bid on the date with you."

The sound of his name sent that same jolt of excitement, anger, and hurt coursing through her that she'd felt when she'd seen him. "I had no idea he was going to be there."

Melanie grimaced. "I'm sorry, Ash. I'm sure it wasn't easy to see him. And to have him spend five *thousand* dollars to go out to dinner with you?" She shook her head. "What was *that* all about?"

Ashleigh had been wondering the same thing from the moment it had happened.

Her phone chimed a text. She looked at the screen. It was from Chase. Heart pounding, she read the message.

I'm sorry about what happened. You can still back out if you want.

She held the phone up for her sister to see.

Melanie scowled. "Now he's trying to get out of it? What a jerk."

Ashleigh set the phone on the cushion beside her. "He tried to back out of it when I talked to him afterwards, but I told him he had to go through with it." She frowned. "Why did I do that?"

Melanie offered a bemused smile. "Yes. Why *did* you do that? Could it be that you still have feelings for him?"

Even if she did—and she wasn't admitting that she did— she wasn't about to say it out loud. Opting to ignore Melanie's question, she picked up her phone. "What should I do?"

Melanie's eyebrows rose. "I say go for it. Why not? I mean, you could pepper him with questions about his life, discover that he's miserable without you, and then move on knowing he got what he deserved when he left you all those years ago."

That sounded appealing. With a wicked grin, Ashleigh tapped in her reply. *No backing out. When I make a commitment, I stick with it.* She showed the message to Melanie, who nodded her endorsement, then Ashleigh hit Send.

Chase replied immediately. *Great! How about tomorrow night?*

Ashleigh sucked in a mouthful of air which stuck in her throat, making her cough uncontrollably.

"Are you okay?" Melanie asked, patting her on the back.

"Yeah," she choked out. "Yeah, I'm fine."

"What did he say?"

"He wants to go out tomorrow night."

Melanie nodded with solemn wisdom. "He wants to get it over with."

Annoyed now, Ashleigh pursed her lips. "Thanks, Mel."

Melanie laughed and shook her head. "Are you going to accept?"

Ashleigh lifted her chin. "Yeah. But only because *I* want to get it over with."

Smirking, Melanie stood. "Right. Well, I'm going to bed."

Staring at her phone, Ashleigh said, "'Night." Then she typed in *Fine* before pressing Send. Not the most enthusiastic response, but it was the best she could do.

Chase replied right away. *Perfect! Let's meet at The Glasshouse Restaurant at six.*

That was one of the few places in Emerald Falls she and Chase hadn't gone to together during the year they'd dated. Thankfully. She didn't think she could tolerate spending an evening with him in a place that held memories. Being with him at all would be hard enough.

She replied with a thumb's up emoji, then headed to bed.

CHAPTER 9

*A*shleigh got to the restaurant twenty minutes late. It was out of character for her to not be on time, and it had been hard to let the clock run out before leaving her house, but it had been a calculated move. Why? Because she wanted Chase to have to wait for her and wonder if she was going to show up. It was dumb and childish, but she needed to show him that *she* was in charge, that she was doing him a favor by gracing him with her presence. When he'd dumped her and left town, she'd been deeply hurt. It was his turn to feel... *something.*

She strode to the front door of the The Glasshouse knowing she looked amazing in her form-fitting sapphire blue, thigh-high dress that showed off her figure and matched her eyes perfectly, plus her five inch heels that she rarely wore because she felt like she might fall over when she walked but they lengthened her legs so she had to wear them. She imagined Chase's expression when he saw her and suppressed a grin.

A greeter opened the door for her. She sauntered inside, stopping in front of the hostess. "I'm meeting someone. Chase Matthews."

The hostess ran her finger down a list of names. "Ah yes." She smiled at Ashleigh. "He made a reservation, but I'm afraid he's not here yet."

Completely deflated that her being late ploy had utterly failed, she felt her shoulders droop. Once again, he'd let her down.

"Would you like to be seated?"

Pushing a smile onto her lips—after all, she still looked amazing even if Chase wasn't there to see her grand entrance—she nodded. "Sure."

"Please follow me."

With a feeling of resignation that this evening wasn't going to go the way she'd planned, Ashleigh trailed after the hostess, almost tripping once, but she made it to the table without incident, then slid into the chair the hostess swept her arm toward. The hostess left her with the promise that her server would be arriving soon. With her eyes on the entrance, Ashleigh tried to guess what could be so important that Chase would be late for their date. Or could it be that he was playing the same game she had been? If so, he was obviously better at it.

Moments later he walked into the restaurant, his expression harried. He spoke to the hostess, but his eyes were sweeping the restaurant, and when they landed on Ashleigh, he broke into a smile, said something to the hostess, and strode to the table.

"Hey," he said when he reached her. "I'm sorry I'm late. I had—"

Ashleigh held up her hand, cutting him off. "It's fine. I *just* got here myself."

This earned her raised eyebrows—after all, he knew she was always punctual. He didn't reply. Instead, he sat in the seat across from her. "Good." He looked toward the server near them before turning back to Ashleigh. "So, you haven't ordered anything yet?"

"No. I *just* got here." Was she belaboring the point? Dang it, she wished she'd gotten there five minutes later.

"Right." He motioned for the server to come to their table.

Christmas music played softly in the background, and as Ashleigh waited for the server to make his way to their table, she surreptitiously took inventory of Chase. Tousled thick brown hair. Check. Piercing green eyes. Check. Full, kissable lips—she knew from experience just how kissable those lips were. Check. Broad shoulders and well-defined biceps. Check. Check.

"Ma'am?" the server asked her.

Tearing her eyes from Chase's biceps, she glanced at him and knew he'd caught her checking him out. Dang it! She jerked her gaze to the server. "Just ice water for me, please."

The server left, leaving the two of them alone.

"Your fundraiser seemed to go well," Chase said.

Oh, man. Why did he have to bring *that* up? "Yeah. I'm happy with it." *Except the part where Taylor put me on the auction block.*

"Did you raise the money you'd hoped to raise?"

Really? After he'd given five thousand dollars? Was he fishing for a compliment?

"Yeah," she said as the server set their drinks in front of them. She took a sip of water, swallowing her pride along with the cold liquid. "Thanks in large part to you."

A grin lit his face. "Glad I could help."

I'll bet you are. And, boy, it's weird sitting across from you having a conversation like nothing happened between us.

"What are you going to use the money for?"

This was a topic she could discuss without feeling the rancor toward him that seemed to keep pushing at her. "I want to get more computers so that patrons don't have to wait so long to use one, and the audiobook department desperately needs to be beefed up. Not to mention the need for more print books." Should she mention her dream project? The one that seemed completely out of reach? The one she'd only told Taylor about?

"What else?"

Slightly embarrassed by the craziness of it, she softly chuckled. "You'll think this is nuts."

He shook his head. "Try me."

He seemed genuinely interested, so why not tell him?

"Okay. There are a lot of patrons who live a bit far out and don't have transportation. If I could raise enough money to buy a Bookmobile, that would be... well, it would be amazing."

He nodded. "That would be something. And I'm sure a lot of people would benefit from that." He smiled. "I'm really impressed by all that you're doing."

He seemed sincere, which made her soften toward him. "Thanks." Too bad she would never raise enough money. The cost for a used Bookmobile was close to a hundred thousand dollars and a new one could run triple that. It was something to reach for, even if she never quite made it.

The server returned and they ordered their food.

"So, Chase, why are you in town?" In all the years they'd been apart, she'd never seen him around town. Whether that was because he hardly came to town or just dumb luck, she didn't know, although she suspected it was the former. When he'd left he'd made it clear that his future lay elsewhere. Forcing her thoughts away from the past and back to the present, she waited to hear his answer.

"Just here to visit my family for Christmas."

"Really? I mean, Christmas is nearly three weeks away. Don't you have a business to run?"

He grinned. "You know about my business?"

Dang it! She needed to try thinking before speaking. "Not really," she said to cover the fact that she'd stalked him on social media and had checked out his company's website more than once. "What is it you do, exactly?"

"My firm is all about cybersecurity."

She gave him a perplexed look, like she had no idea what that meant, although she'd Googled it the first time she'd read it. "Tell me more."

He launched into an explanation about what his company did—protecting computer systems, networks, and programs from attack. His eyes sparkled with enthusiasm as he spoke. Ashleigh couldn't help but stare at his animated features. He obviously loved what he did as much as she loved what she did. Maybe she'd been too hard on him when he'd left town to follow his dreams.

Then she reminded herself that after he'd shattered her heart, he hadn't reached out to her, not once. Passion or not, he could have at least asked how she was doing.

With her anger rekindled, she schooled her expression. Needing a distraction, she glanced around for the server, who thankfully was bringing their food.

CHAPTER 10

The blue of Ashleigh's dress set off her eyes and really grabbed Chase's attention. Not that it took much for her to grab his attention, much to his consternation. When she'd insisted that he follow through with this date, he'd planned on having dinner, saying goodnight, and moving on with his life. But now, with her sitting across from him being so attentive, her intelligent eyes appraising him, her beautiful face bringing back all kinds of memories... He already knew he was going to ask her out again. Whether or not she would agree was another question entirely, but he had to give it a shot.

The server set their food in front of them. He began eating, then paused and lifted his gaze. "Ashleigh?"

She looked up from her salad.

"I, uh, I was wondering what you're doing tomorrow."

She narrowed her eyes. "Why?"

That wasn't the response he'd expected. Then again, what *had* he expected? For her to fall all over herself to be with him? Why would she do that after the way he'd left her? Even so, he had to give this a shot. "I thought it might be fun to catch up."

She tilted her head. "Isn't that what we're doing now?"

He was an idiot. Okay, maybe he wasn't. After all, he was one of *Silicon Valley's 30 under 30 to Watch.* But when it came to women, he was definitely an idiot.

Scrambling to come up with a better answer, it occurred to him that maybe he could tell the truth—that he wanted to spend more time with her. "Yes, that is what we're doing now and I'm really enjoying it. Aren't you?"

She pursed her lips like she was trying to figure out if she was. "I haven't decided yet."

"Okay. That's fair. We haven't seen each other in a long time."

That earned him a frown. "It's been six years, Chase."

He knew that. "Right."

"Six years without a single word from you." Her frown deepened. "That hurt."

Why had it never occurred to him to contact her all those years? He truly was an idiot. "I know this probably doesn't help, but I want you to know that I'm sorry."

"About what, exactly?"

Oh boy. Softly sighing, he said, "About the way I left and that I never reached out to you."

She frowned. "I accept your apology."

Hold on. He'd broken up with her. Didn't that mean they were supposed to cut all ties? Did ex-boyfriends normally keep in touch after a break up? Was apologizing even the right thing to do? "Even though I didn't reach out to you, we both went on with our lives and everything was fine, right?"

Her eyebrows jerked together, which was when he realized he'd taken out a shovel that should have been kept stowed and had started digging. Even so, he couldn't seem to stop himself. "I know I accomplished a ton over the last six years, and it looks you did too." *Shut up, Chase. Just shut the heck up.* "If I'd stayed in Emerald Falls, I never would have been as successful as I am. So, really, it's good I left."

Deep frown lines appeared on Ashleigh's forehead, which was when Chase managed to set the shovel aside for a tiny break before he picked it up and attempted to fill the hole he'd dug. "You know what? Forget what I just said. I'm an idiot."

What did he mean it was good that he'd left? It was true that if he'd stayed he probably wouldn't have been able to build his company like he had, but there was more to life than making money. There was love and relationships and loyalty. Things he clearly had no inkling about.

Ashleigh kept her lips clamped shut. If she opened them, she would say things she couldn't take back and would later regret. Then she thought of something she could say, something that might get through to him without destroying the shred of...whatever it was...they had going.

She smiled sweetly. "You're right. It's good you left."

His eyebrows shot up. "Really?"

"Mm-hmm. That allowed me to figure out that you weren't the right man for me." Which, she was certain, had nothing to do with the fact that six years later she was still single.

Slowly nodding, like he wasn't sure if this was a trick, he said, "Okay."

Ignoring him, she concentrated on her salad, trying to savor every bite, but she couldn't taste a thing as memories of him breaking up with her washed over her. When he'd told her that there was nothing for him in Emerald Falls— after they'd been dating for a year!—that had obviously included her. To him, *she* was nothing. But she had believed they were *something*. She'd been in love with him. In her mind they would be together forever. When he'd left, she had been inconsolable.

"Ashleigh," he said, his voice soft.

Tears threatened to fill her eyes. Blinking furiously to keep them at bay, when she'd gotten her emotions under control, she lifted her gaze to look at him. But dang it, with him sitting right across from her, all of those feelings crashed over her again.

She'd *loved* him. So much. And he'd dumped her without a second thought. Why, if it hurt so much, was she sitting with him and listening to him tell her that leaving had been a good thing?

She had to put some space between them. About to excuse herself, when she saw tears fill his eyes and he said, "My mom is dying," all the anger and hurt fled.

CHAPTER 11

*C*hase didn't know why he'd blurted that out. Hadn't he done enough damage for one evening? Why did he feel the need to share something so painful? It wasn't like Ashleigh could do anything about his mom's illness.

Ashleigh stared at him, her eyebrows furrowed. "What?"

"I'm sorry." That was, what? The third time he'd apologized since he'd gotten there? A new record. "I shouldn't have laid that on you."

"No. I mean, I'm glad you told me. I always liked your mom." Her eyes softened. "How long does she have?"

Chase shook his head. "I don't know. She had cancer a few years ago, and it's, well, it's back and it's spread." Sadness swept over him. "It's not looking good." He cleared his throat. "We're starting hospice care."

Ashleigh reached her hand across the table and placed it on his. "I'm so sorry, Chase."

The touch of her warm, soft hand filled him with unexpected longing and all of a sudden Chase wanted to go back six years and make a different choice. A choice that kept Ashleigh in his life.

Wanting to distract himself from his unexpected feelings, he said, "We'll get through it."

She pulled her hand away and nodded. "You will. Plus, you have Jordyn."

Yes, he had his sister, and that was incredibly important, but he realized he wanted more than that—someone for him to love in a different way than a sister. And to be loved back. "Yeah."

"Is there anything I can do?"

Was there? He couldn't think of anything. "No. But thank you for asking." Ready to turn the conversation away from his sad news, he said, "Tell me what else is going on in your life."

She was quiet a moment, then she smirked. "Like, who I'm dating?"

The thought of her dating other men bothered him, although he was curious. "Yeah. Sure."

Should she make up a dream man? Pretend like she was having the time of her life? It was tempting, although what good that would do was debatable. Chase was in Emerald Falls to spend time with his mom, obviously. It had been coincidental that he'd come to the fundraiser. If it hadn't been for that, she wouldn't have known he was in town.

"You don't want to know about my love life, Chase." Mainly because she didn't have one. Not with the man-fast she'd put herself on. She would have asked herself why she was on this date then, except it hadn't been her choice. The blame fell squarely on Taylor, who she would get back in a way she had to devise. "What about you?"

"What about me?" he asked, one side of his mouth quirking up like he knew exactly what she was asking.

Wait. She didn't want to know about his love life. Not when she already did know—thanks to all the pictures she'd seen on social media. "Never mind."

His smile faded like he was disappointed not to be able to share.

What a jerk. Why would she want to know about all the women he'd gone out with?

Suddenly she did want to know. At least know if there was anyone he was serious with. But if he was, why would he have bid on this date? With all kinds of questions flying through her mind, she said, "Are you dating anyone?"

"I've dated a few women, but no one I'm really into."

"What kind of woman would you be into?" Why on earth was she asking that? She didn't care who he dated. Did she?

With a thoughtful look, he took a sip of his drink. "I want a woman I'm attracted to, of course, but also someone I can have an intelligent conversation with and laugh with."

Didn't that fit her exactly? If so, why had he left her? Frustrated, she decided to change the subject. "What do you like to do in your free time?"

Even as Chase described his perfect woman, he knew he was describing Ashleigh. With time and distance, he'd come to realize that she was so much more interesting and so much better than the women he'd been wasting his time with. More than ever, he wanted to set up a second date.

"I've been pretty busy with my business," he began, "but when I have time for fun, I like to play softball or go on bike rides or go camping and hiking. And in the winter I like to snowboard."

"Emerald Falls has a co-ed softball team. Gage was the coach last season."

Chase remembered playing in Emerald Falls back in the day. "Nice." He paused a beat. "Do you ever go snowboarding?" When they'd dated, they'd never gone.

"I've been a few times, but it's been a while."

This was his opening. "Would you like to go tomorrow?"

She gazed at him. "That might be difficult."

She hadn't flatly refused, so that was promising. "Why's that?"

"I don't have a snowboard."

Was that all? He could easily solve that problem. "What if I got you the gear you needed?"

She tilted her head. "Why would you do that?"

Why was she making this so difficult? Okay, she had every right to. Still, it would be nice if she made it a little easier. "Consider it a Christmas present."

Offering a bemused smile, she said, "Chase. We haven't exchanged Christmas presents since you left."

The server cleared their salad plates and set their entrees on the table.

"Look, Ashleigh, all I want is to go snowboarding—or anything else—with you."

She pursed her lips. "Taylor might have a snowboard and other gear I can borrow."

His eyebrows shot up. "Are you saying you'll go with me?"

Her shoulders lifted in a shrug. "Why not?"

One of the least enthusiastic responses he'd ever received when asking a woman out, but he'd take it. "Great!" Already, his mind was racing with the possible things he could do to impress her. Then he asked himself why he was so eager to dazzle her. It had been a long time since they'd dated. He didn't even live in Emerald Falls. Why was he making such an effort? But he knew why. Because being with Ashleigh had rekindled all kinds of feelings he was having trouble suppressing. Even more startling, he didn't want to suppress them.

They finished their meal as they caught up on their lives,

and when Chase told Ashleigh goodnight, he found himself eager to see her the next day.

When he got home, his mom was sitting in the living room watching TV. She muted the volume and asked how the date had gone, her eyes alight with hope, although her face was drawn and pale.

Worried about her, he sat on the couch beside her and smiled. "Much better than I thought it would."

"Good." She paused. "Are you going out again?"

Picturing Ashley's subdued excitement, he softly chuckled. "Yes. Tomorrow, as a matter of fact."

She smiled brightly. "See? I knew it would work out."

Chase wasn't sure anything had worked out yet, but his mom seemed so happy at the thought that he and Ashleigh were dating again that he didn't want to say anything to dash her joy. "Time will tell, Mom."

She touched his arm. "You and Ashleigh are meant to be together, Chase."

The thought startled him. "What?"

She nodded. "It wasn't a coincidence what happened at the fundraiser."

Hmm. He wasn't sure about that, but he let her comment ride.

"Nothing would make me happier than to see you with the right woman." She nodded to emphasize her point. "Someone with a good head on her shoulders." Her eyes and voice softened. "Someone who would be a good wife to you and a good mother to my grandchildren." Tears filled her eyes. "I would die happy if I knew you had found such a woman." She sniffed. "I know I might not live to see you get married, but if you were at least engaged..." Her words trailed off.

He didn't like her talking about dying. She was his only parent and the thought of losing her devastated him. Still, he was realistic. He knew this time there was a high likelihood that the cancer would win. It was too far gone.

Softly chuckling, he said, "No pressure, huh, Mom?"

She smiled. "I'm sorry, Chase. I've just been feeling melancholy lately." Still, she didn't retract her challenge.

CHAPTER 12

"I have to admit, Ash," Melanie said the next morning as Ashleigh got ready, "I'm kind of surprised you agreed to a second date with Chase. I mean, I really thought last night's date would be it."

So had she, but evidently she'd had a moment of weakness when she'd agreed to go. She could always cancel, but surprisingly, she didn't want to. "What about you? Are you and Gage getting together today?"

Smiling happily, Melanie nodded. "Yep. He's taking Avery and me bowling."

"That'll be fun."

"Yeah. It will be Avery's first time, so she's pretty excited. In fact, I'd better go wake her up."

Ashleigh envied the relationship Melanie had with Gage. They'd been dating for a number of months and were really into each other. Ashleigh hoped one day she could find a man to love her the way Gage loved Melanie.

As she got ready, Ashleigh thought about her conversation with Taylor the evening before. She'd stopped by Taylor's house on the way home from her date with Chase to explain what she needed. Taylor's eyebrows couldn't have gone any higher into her hairline. "Does this mean you're not mad at me anymore?"

Ashleigh had snorted a laugh. "That's yet to be determined."

With a smirk, Taylor had said, "Guess your man-fast is over, huh?"

"It's just one date. My man-fast can start again on Monday."

Taylor gave her a look that said she would believe it when she saw it.

Softly chuckling, Ashleigh said, "Stop. Can I borrow your gear or not?"

"Of course. Anything to help you with your new man."

"He is not my new man."

Taylor turned away to get the gear. "We'll see."

Now, as Ashleigh replayed the conversation, she wondered why she was breaking her man-fast already. Was it because she was intrigued by the fact that Chase was so eager to go out with her? Or maybe she needed this time with him to give herself closure on their relationship. Maybe it was a little of both, although she had to ask herself if she was a little bit nuts for agreeing to it. Between the nearly two-hour drive to get to the ski resort and the hours of snowboarding they would do, their date would last most of the day.

Or maybe she just liked to torture herself.

No matter. She'd agreed to go out with him, and since Taylor had loaned her the gear she needed, she was all set. She found herself actually looking forward to this date. Partly because she hadn't been snowboarding in quite a while, and partly because she would be able to spend time with Chase. Okay, maybe those parts weren't equally divided.

Ashleigh finished getting ready and a short time later the doorbell rang.

Heart leaping with unexpected anticipation, Ashleigh glided to the door and opened it. Chase stood on the porch, a jaunty smile on his lips. He wore snowboard pants and a sweater that fit him in a way that emphasized his tall, muscular body. He looked good. There was no denying that.

"Hello," he said, his gaze going up and down Ashleigh's body, sending a thrill of excitement through her. "Looks like you're wearing the right gear to go snowboarding."

Ashleigh glanced down at her snowboarding pants—also borrowed from Taylor. "I'm ready to do this."

He smiled. "Looks like you were able to get the equipment."

Ashleigh turned and looked at the snowboard, bindings, and boots tucked in the entryway. "Yep. I picked up all the gear from Taylor last evening."

"Perfect. Let's load up and we'll get going." Chase scooped up all of the gear, and after Ashleigh put on a warm coat, she followed him out the door and to a Jeep parked in her driveway.

"Is this your Jeep?" she asked, taking in the sleek black color.

He laughed. "No. Jordyn traded me cars for the day."

"That was nice of her."

Chase softly chuckled and shook his head.

"What?"

He secured the snowboard to the roof rack and turned to Ashleigh. "It was her idea."

Thinking his sister was very thoughtful, Ashleigh shrugged, then when Chase held open the passenger door, she climbed inside. Chase got behind the wheel and they backed out of Ashleigh's driveway.

As they made the trip to the ski resort Chase had selected, Ashleigh marveled at where she was at that moment. Only days earlier if someone had told her she would go on two dates in two days with Chase Matthews, she would have told them they were certifiable, yet here she was, alone with the one man who had broken her heart and who she'd never been able to get out of her mind.

Taking in his masculine profile, Ashleigh felt a little flutter in her belly.

"What are you thinking about?" Chase asked, catching her off guard.

Should she admit the truth? What the heck? At least part of it. "Just how crazy it is that I'm here with you."

One side of his mouth quirked up as he glanced at her. "Really? Why is it so crazy?"

"Just, you know, who would have thought we'd be spending time together at this point in our lives?"

He chuckled. "Right?" He glanced at her. "And both of us single."

And why was that? Ashleigh thought she knew her reason— she had trust issues. And she placed the blame for those issues squarely on Chase's shoulders. She'd been in love with him, had believed they were destined to be married. And then he'd left her. Would she ever get over that? Who knew, but maybe spending this time with him would help. And then maybe they could be friends. Despite her lingering attraction to him.

"Why are you still single, Ashleigh?" Chase asked, putting an end to her quiet musings.

"That's none of your business," she snapped, shocking herself with the vehemence of her answer.

He threw his hands up in mock surrender. "Okay, okay. Forget I asked."

Embarrassed, she backpedaled. "I'm sorry. That was uncalled for."

He glanced her way. "Not necessarily. I mean, we haven't spoken in years. You don't owe me any explanations."

Grateful he wasn't making her feel any smaller than she already did, she relaxed. Still, she wasn't about to tell him her real reasons. "I'm not comfortable talking about my love life with you."

He nodded. "Okay. That's fine." He smiled at her. "Let's talk about something completely unrelated to love lives."

Relieved he wasn't making a big deal about it, she smiled. "Like what?"

"Like, how well did you do the last time you went snowboarding?"

She smiled. "Not too bad, although I do have lots of room for improvement."

They talked about the finer points of snowboarding and other non-love life related topics, and when they reached the ski resort, they unloaded their gear and made their way to the ticket line. Soon, they were riding a chairlift up the mountain.

Ashleigh was kind of nervous to go on her first run after such a long time.

"Are you okay?" Chase asked. "You're so quiet."

She studied his handsome face, his green eyes shining with sincere interest. "Just a little nervous."

He smiled, then placed his gloved hand over hers. "I'll stay right with you the entire time."

Would he though? It was hard to believe him after he'd bailed on her six years earlier.

Wanting to think of something else, she focused on the feel of his hand on hers. Though the fabric of their gloves kept her from feeling his skin, the weight of his hand still sent a jolt of longing through her body. She missed him. So much. Too bad she needed to keep him firmly in her past—at least a romantic version of him. There was no way she could risk letting him in just so he could shatter her heart a second time.

Wanting to put him firmly in the zone of friendship, she pulled her hand away. "I'm sure I'll be fine on my own."

"I'm sure you would be, but I'd like to stay with you."

Why was he saying that? Confused, Ashleigh tossed him a small smile, then watched as they neared the top of the mountain.

CHAPTER 13

*C*hase's feelings were coming fast and strong, which was a problem he hadn't anticipated. He'd only wanted to enjoy some time with Ashleigh, not resurrect feelings that he'd thought were long dead. Yet here he was, his heart betraying him. Then the brief but powerful conversation he'd had with his mom the night before flashed into his mind.

He gave Ashleigh a sideways glance. Did his mom really believe the two of them were meant to be together? He wasn't so sure himself, although he was willing to entertain the idea. Then again, what did Ashleigh think? Did she still hold the way he'd left Emerald Falls and her against him? She was on this date, which was promising, but he had no idea what she was really thinking.

They reached the end of the chairlift ride and hopped off before making their way to the beginning of the run.

Chase needed to stop overthinking things and just enjoy himself. That's why they were there.

"Are you ready?" he asked Ashleigh, who seemed more certain now that she was on the snow.

Smiling brightly, she nodded. "Yeah. Let's do this."

With that, she took off and Chase followed. She was doing pretty well. Much better than she'd let on.

Moments later she fell. He raced to her side but found her laughing, her eyes bright with enjoyment. Something about the happiness she exuded drew him in and all of a sudden he wanted to kiss her.

Slow down, Chase.

"Are you okay?" he asked as memories of kissing her years ago filled his mind.

Softly chuckling, she nodded. "Yeah. Just lost my footing."

He helped her up and they continued down the hill.

When they reached the bottom, they immediately got back on the chairlift and did another run, this time without either one of them falling. They did several more runs before Chase suggested they stop for a lunch break.

"Sounds good to me," Ashleigh said. "I'm starving."

Hoisting their snowboards over their shoulders, they made their way to the cafe, stowing their boards in a locker before going inside.

"Mmm," Ashleigh said, "smells delicious."

Chase perused the menu posted on the wall. "Don't tell me. You want pizza."

She laughed. "Yep."

"We can split one. Just like the old days."

At the mention of their past, Ashleigh's smile dimmed. "Right."

Wanting to lift the mood, he asked what kind she wanted.

"I'm good with whatever, just—"

"No onions?"

She smiled and nodded.

He ordered a ham and pineapple, then they went to a booth to wait for their food.

"How's your mom doing?" Ashleigh asked.

"About the same." Although the previous night she'd seemed weaker than he'd seen her before, and the in-home hospice care had started that day, which made it all seem so much more serious. The conversation he'd had with his mom the night before came to mind, the one where she'd said she would die happy if he was engaged.

Was that even possible? How much time did she have? What if she only lived another month? There was no way he could become engaged in such a short period of time, right? He lifted his gaze to Ashleigh and a crazy idea popped into his head. But would she go for it? No, it was too nuts.

Ashleigh was having a blast with Chase. The morning had

been nothing but light and fun. Until he'd said they could split a pizza like in the old days. The reminder of their past had sent an arrow of pain right to her heart. But she'd shaken if off. She had to leave the past where it belonged and focus on the here and now. She would be ultra-careful to guard her heart, but she could enjoy herself while doing that.

Of course, now that they were sitting across from each other without the distraction of snowboarding down a mountain, she had to face her confused feelings. On the one hand she wanted to keep Chase firmly in the zone of friendship, but on the other, she still cared deeply for him in a more-than-friends way.

She lifted her eyes to his. Why did he have a funny look on his face? "What's wrong?"

His eyes briefly widened like he hadn't realized she knew him so well that she could easily read his expression. "Uh…" He chuckled. "Nothing's wrong. It's just, I had an idea."

Curious, she tilted her head. "What idea?"

He rubbed at one of his ears. "I don't know if I should tell you."

That piqued her curiosity even more, although she worried he was just going to suggest another date. She'd already decided that she couldn't continue seeing him. Yes, she wanted to be friends with him, but they needed to slow this down. Two dates in two days was too much when she wanted to tamp down her feelings for him. She had to make her wishes clear. "It's not another date, is it?"

Running a hand through his hair, he said, "Not exactly."

That was a relief. But he seemed kind of agitated. What was going on?

"Here's your pizza," a woman said as she set the steaming pie on the table between them. "Enjoy."

"Thank you," Chase said, then he pulled a slice from the pan and slid it onto his plate.

Ashleigh ignored the pizza, her gaze locked on Chase. "Don't leave me hanging. I want to hear this idea."

He stared at the slice of pizza on his plate for several seconds, then he met her gaze. "It's more of a proposition."

Eyebrows furrowing, Ashleigh asked, "What do you mean?"

"You know how sick my mom is."

"Yeah."

He got quiet for a moment like he was trying to contain his emotions. "Today she started in-home hospice."

That was serious. "Oh."

He nodded. "Last night she told me she has only one wish before she, well, before she dies." He went quiet again, which touched Ashleigh. She and Melanie had lost both of their parents to a car accident when they'd been in elementary school so she knew how awful it was to lose a parent. She knew Chase's mom meant everything to him, especially since his father was not in his life. Losing her would be devastating.

"What's her wish?" Her voice was soft as she asked.

He took a long swallow of his soda before setting his

glass down and clearing his throat. "She wants me to be engaged."

What in the world was he talking about? And why did that involve a proposition to *her*?

Oh. Oh! As the implication hit her, her heart nearly stopped beating and a million emotions roiled through her.

CHAPTER 14

Chase knew his idea was crazy, so why was he pressing forward with it?

But he knew why. The thought of losing his mom tore him to shreds. The least he could do was make her dying wish come true before the cancer took her life. And if that meant she believed he was happily engaged, he wanted to make it happen. Sure, he could pretend with one of the women he knew at home in Cupertino, but that wouldn't be good enough. His mom wanted him to be engaged to someone she approved of, and the only woman who fit that bill was Ashleigh. However, at the look on Ashleigh's face—eyes as wide as a deer who was standing in the road with a semi-truck bearing down on it—he wasn't sure he should complete his explanation.

"What do you mean, Chase? What are you saying?"

It was too late. He had to explain. Even if she laughed in his face or got up and left.

"What if," he began, "we pretended to be engaged? Just for show, to, you know, convince my mom that I'm on my way to getting married." Emotion clogged his throat. "That's the *only* thing she wants."

Guilt plowed through Ashleigh because she had to say no. She couldn't do this. More than anything, she didn't want to. How could she after all Chase had put her through? How dare he even ask? But his mom was dying. It was terribly sad, but it was asking too much for her to do this, to pretend she and Chase were in love and ready to get married.

At the look of unadulterated hope in his eyes, she hated to tell him her answer. Nevertheless, she had to.

"I'm sorry, Chase, but I can't do that."

His expression fell as his shoulders drooped. He looked down and started massaging his temples.

Seeing him like this tugged at Ashleigh's heart. This was obviously something he wanted very badly, but something she couldn't give him. He'd hurt her too much in the past. She couldn't risk her heart again. Even though it would be for pretend, she knew herself well enough to know that in her heart it would be all too real. It would be the future she'd envisioned when she and Chase had been dating six years earlier.

Chase lifted his eyes and stared at her. "What can I do to convince you?"

She shook her head as guilt washed over her again. "Nothing, Chase. The answer is no."

He was silent a moment, then in a soft voice he said, "You would be her Christmas Angel, Ashleigh."

Oh man. Why did he have to put it that way? That just made her feel even more guilty. And, for a minute, it even made her consider saying yes.

Not quite ready to agree, she stared at the table in front of her.

"How badly do you want that Bookmobile?"

Her head snapped up. Chase was smiling.

He wasn't really going to tempt her with an outrageous offer, was he? Of course he was. He knew how important that Bookmobile was to her—a pipe dream, but a dream nonetheless. Something she didn't believe she could ever acquire. Not with the funds she'd raised so far and ever had the hope of raising, but something she would dearly love to have for their little library.

He didn't wait for her to answer. "If you pretend to be my fiancée I will buy the library a brand-new Bookmobile."

Ashleigh gasped. She couldn't help it. A brand-new Bookmobile was hundreds of thousands of dollars. Was Chase insane? "You're joking, right?"

His smile grew, maybe because he believed she was entertaining his absurd offer. "No. I'm completely serious."

She didn't want to insult him, but before she could even

think about agreeing to this—and she was a long way from saying yes—she needed to know if he could actually afford it. "You know how much a new one costs, right?"

His expression was light, like this was no big deal, like he dropped crazy amounts of cash all the time. "Yeah. I know."

"And you have the money?"

He grinned. "I have the money."

Wow. His business was doing better than she thought.

"So, you'll do it?"

His assumption that she could be bought off with a Bookmobile ticked her off, even if it might be true. Her eyebrows yanked together. "I didn't say that."

The smile melted from his face. "Oh."

They were both silent for several beats.

She needed time to think about this, time to decide how badly she wanted that Bookmobile versus how much risk she was willing to take for her heart. And then there was Sheila, Chase's mom. Ashleigh had always liked her, and of course she wanted to be her Christmas Angel, but could she really do this? The reasons to do it were piling up, but her mind still rebelled against the idea, rejecting it hard.

Taking a slice of pizza from the pan, she said, "The pizza's getting cold."

Chase had been so sure that offering to buy a Bookmobile would seal the deal, but Ashleigh had shut that assumption right down. Chest tightening on disappointment, he lifted his slice of pizza and took a bite. He would make the best of this. Obviously, he couldn't always get what he wanted, even if it was a worthy desire. Even if he had more money than he knew what to do with.

They ate in silence, both lost in thought. Chase hoped Ashleigh was considering his idea, but he would resist the temptation to push. In fact, he would drop the subject and not ask her again.

When the pizza was gone, Chase smiled at Ashleigh. "Ready to do more snowboarding?"

She looked a little surprised that he'd moved on from his proposition—looked relieved, actually. Good. No reason to ruin the good time they were having with pressure to agree to his proposed idea. Either she would do it or she wouldn't. He'd made his offer. Now it was up to her to decide.

"Sure," she said as she got to her feet. "I think I still have a few runs left in me."

"Awesome! Let's hit it."

CHAPTER 15

*A*shleigh was mildly surprised Chase hadn't asked her again about being his fake fiancée. While they'd eaten it had been all she could think about. She'd mentally listed the pros and cons of agreeing to his ridiculous idea and had begun to think maybe it wasn't as ridiculous as she'd first imagined. Although if she agreed to it she would have a lot of rules.

They rode the chairlift up the mountain and made another run, but she was having trouble concentrating as her mind kept going to Chase's proposition. Truthfully, it wasn't even the Bookmobile that pressed on her mind—although that would be beyond amazing—it was Sheila. If her dying wish was to see Chase happily engaged and Ashleigh could make that happen, how selfish was she to deny her that?

Maybe I should do it.

The thought jolted her. Was she actually considering saying yes to this ludicrous scheme?

Yes. Yes, she was.

An image of Sheila from the night of the fundraiser filled Ashleigh's mind, closely followed by how nice Sheila had always been to Ashleigh when she had dated Chase all those years earlier. Ashleigh couldn't count the number of times Sheila had had Ashleigh over for family dinners. Sheila had overcome a lot in her life and now she had a terminal illness and all she wanted was for her son to be happy. And Ashleigh could be her Christmas Angel.

Tears flooded Ashleigh's eyes, making it impossible to see the run clearly. She lost her balance and fell to the snow. Fortunately, she'd reached the end of the run. Almost immediately, Chase was there asking if she was okay and helping her to her feet.

She got her emotions under control, but her eyes were wet. Removing her goggles, she swiped at her eyes with her gloved hand, which did little to hide the fact that she'd been crying.

Chase's forehead furrowed. "What's wrong?"

"I'll do it," she said, her voice soft.

"Do what?" A moment later he must have figured out what she was talking about because his face lit up, but half a beat later the worry was back. "Are you sure? I mean, if it makes you that upset I'm not going to ask you to do it."

Touched by his thoughtfulness, she laughed. "I wasn't crying because of that."

"Oh." He paused. "Then why were you crying?"

"I was thinking about your mom. About how I can make her dying wish come true."

This seemed to take him aback as his eyes suddenly shone with unshed tears, but he smiled and nodded. "She'll be so happy when we tell her we're..." He began coughing like he'd just realized what he was about to do.

"You okay?" Ashleigh asked when his coughing fit went on for several seconds.

He nodded, finally getting himself under control. "Yeah. I'm good."

"Are you having second thoughts?" In a way, she hoped he was because she still had plenty of misgivings.

"No."

Alrighty then.

He tilted his head. "Are you?"

Yes. Plenty of them, but she would do this for his mother—and for that wonderful Bookmobile. She would just have to make sure her heart understood it was all pretend.

Chase couldn't believe Ashleigh had actually agreed to be his fake fiancée. When he'd presented the idea to her he'd been hopeful she would agree, although he'd had his doubts. But now? Now they were going to pretend to the world that they were engaged.

"We need to set some ground rules," she said, dragging him back to the present.

"Ground rules? Okay, yeah." That made sense. They had to think this through. "Let's go back to the cafe and have some hot chocolate. We can discuss it there."

Ten minutes later they were sitting in a booth away from everyone, steaming mugs of hot chocolate in front of them.

"You go first," he said.

Looking thoughtful, she nodded. "All right. First, no kissing."

What? That was absurd. How would they convince people they were in love and engaged to be married if they never kissed?

Ashleigh must have read the disbelief in his expression because she said, "If you don't agree, Chase, then forget the whole thing. I'm out." She put her hands up as she sat back against the booth.

He had no choice but to agree. Besides, maybe he could change her mind. "Fine. No kissing. But it will be weird."

Her brows furrowed. "How so?"

"Because when we used to date we kissed in front of people all the time."

She shook her head. "People can change. We don't do PDA anymore, that's all."

Chuckling, he lifted his mug, blowing across the surface. "Can we at least hold hands?"

She seemed to consider it. "Okay, yeah. I guess we can at

least do that." She looked at him with sternness. "Once in a while."

That was fine. "Good. What else?"

"Besides holding hands—and that won't be often—no other touching."

He didn't like these rules she was implementing, but what could he do? "All right. Any other rules?"

"I'll let you know when I think of them, but I do have one stipulation."

Holding back a sigh, he smiled. "What's your stipulation?"

"You need to order that Bookmobile tomorrow."

"Don't trust me, huh?"

She raised her eyebrows. "Does it cross my mind that you would run off and leave me hanging? Let me think about that for a millisecond." She tapped her chin, then shook her head. "Nope. I don't trust you."

"That hurts, Ash."

"The truth usually does."

Oh boy. This engagement might be harder than he'd thought it would be.

"Will you order it?" she pressed.

"Yes. As soon as you pick out the one you want."

That earned him a bright smile. "I'll get on that as soon as we get back."

"I have a few rules of my own," he said, then nearly laughed at the look of surprise on her face. What? She thought she was the only one who could come up with rules?

"Okay, what?"

"You can't tell anyone this is fake. Not even Melanie."

"She'll never believe I would get engaged so fast."

Raising his eyebrows, he said, "It's up to you to convince her." To add motivation, he mouthed the word *Bookmobile.*

She rolled her eyes but didn't argue. "When are we going to make our big announcement?"

That was a good question. The sooner the better, as far as he was concerned. But would his mom buy it happening the day after she'd told him it was her dying wish? "We need to go out a few more times before we tell the world. Otherwise it will be harder to sell."

"As long as that Bookmobile is on its way, I'm in."

Thrilled he'd found a way to make this work, Chase suppressed a grin. "Deal."

CHAPTER 16

On the drive home, Ashleigh couldn't stop thinking about the crazy plan she'd agreed to. Then she kept picturing the faces of everyone who knew her. When she told them she and Chase were engaged, they would be shocked. Especially Melanie. Could she convince her sister that she was in love with Chase? Even more, could she convince her that she trusted him enough to marry him?

"What are you thinking about?" Chase asked as they got closer to Emerald Falls.

Softly sighing, she bit her lip. "Just wondering how I'm going to convince Melanie that this is legit."

"Don't worry about that now." He chuckled. "We still have to go out a few more times before we make the big announcement."

Oh yeah. She'd forgotten.

Kind of dreading more dates—the more time she spent with him, the harder it would be to convince her heart it was pretend—she tried to think of a way to minimize her time alone with him. "About that."

"What?" He glanced her way. He must have seen something in her face, because he said, "Don't tell me you're backing out already."

"No. I was just thinking, maybe we should go on a few group dates."

One of his eyebrows arched. "You realize having an audience will require really good acting." He smirked. "And maybe a kiss or two."

She hadn't thought of that. "Never mind then."

This time he cocked his head. "Is kissing me really so abhorrent?"

That was the trouble. Kissing him was the exact opposite of abhorrent. It was delectable. At least in her memory. Every time they'd kissed, she'd fallen for him harder. Which was why she refused to do it now. If her lips touched his... well, it was a chance she simply couldn't take.

Ignoring his question, she looked out her window. "When should we go out again?"

"I don't want to waste any time. Let's go out tomorrow."

She jerked her head around to face him. "Tomorrow?"

He laughed. "If we're going to announce our engagement soon, this needs to be a whirlwind courtship."

Made sense. "Right." She paused. "When *are* we going to announce our engagement?"

"Hmm. How about Friday?"

Her eyes widened. "That's less than a week." She hadn't meant for her voice to nearly squeak.

Chase's forehead creased. "I…I don't know how long my mom has and I want her to have this bit of happiness for as long as she can."

Was Ashleigh being selfish by wanting to put off announcing their fake engagement? On the other hand, maybe it would actually be good to get it out there sooner. Once they announced they were engaged, she could pull back on spending tons of time with him. Right?

She forced a smile. "Friday it is."

A new question flashed into Ashleigh's head, but asking it would sound insensitive. Still, she had to ask. After all, she couldn't put her life on hold forever.

"Chase?"

He looked at her with raised eyebrows.

"How long…that is…how much time should I, uh, plan on for being engaged?"

There, she'd said it. It sounded totally cold and heartless, but it was only fair to know.

What kind of question was that? She was basically asking how long until his mom died. Rather hurt by the idea, the more Chase thought about it, the more he understood her asking. She was doing him a favor—a big one—by agreeing to this charade. It wasn't unreasonable for her to need to know what kind of timeframe they were looking at. Even so, he didn't have an answer.

"I don't know, but I'll tell you what. If you'll commit to two months, then if, with any luck, my mom is still alive at that point, you can walk away with a clear conscience." Chase had to clear his throat to get past the lump that formed.

"I'm sorry, Chase," Ashleigh said as she placed her hand on his.

This time there was no glove between their hands, and the warmth of her soft skin on his sent a jolt of unexpected attraction careening through him.

"I didn't mean to be so insensitive," she said.

Her hand went away, leaving Chase feeling oddly bereft. "I understand. If I were you, I would ask the same question."

"You would?"

He wasn't sure, but if it made her feel better… "Yeah."

She smiled, a look of relief lighting her face.

"So," he asked, "will you commit to two months?" Why did that seem like such a short period of time?

Her eyebrows bunched before smoothing out. "Yes. I can do that."

"Good." He didn't want to have to tell his mom that they'd made the whole thing up, but if it meant she was still alive in two months, then it would be worth it.

They turned onto Ashleigh's street. Chase pulled into her driveway. "What time are you off work tomorrow?"

"Six."

"Okay. I'll pick you up at seven. Does that work for you?"

She hesitated, but only for a moment. "Yeah." At that, she climbed out of the Jeep.

"See you tomorrow."

She nodded but didn't reply.

Clearly, she was reticent about the whole thing, but Chase was eager to see her again.

CHAPTER 17

"We're in the kitchen," Melanie called out the moment Ashleigh walked into the house.

Ashleigh headed straight there, finding her sister and Avery decorating Christmas sugar cookies.

"Looks yummy!" Ashleigh said with a smile.

"How was your date?" Melanie asked as she spread green frosting on a Christmas tree-shaped cookie.

"Aunt Ashy!" Avery shouted, jumping down from her chair and flinging herself at Ashleigh's legs.

Ashleigh scooped up her niece and held her close, giving herself a moment to collect her thoughts before answering Melanie. Her sister knew her so well, would she be able to pull this off?

She would know soon enough.

Setting Avery down, Ashleigh glanced at Melanie. "It was

good." Then she swallowed over the guilt that filled her throat. "We're going out again tomorrow."

Melanie's hands stopped moving as her eyebrows shot up. "What?"

If she and Chase weren't preparing for the fake engagement, would she have said yes to another date? Truthfully, she didn't know. On the one hand, to safeguard her heart she would have had to say no, but on the other, she'd had so much fun snowboarding with Chase that staying home instead didn't sound nearly as enticing.

Not wanting to give anything away—or to lie—she murmured, "Mmm-hmm," then she walked over to the refrigerator and opened the door.

A moment later she felt a tap on her shoulder. She turned to see Melanie standing there with her hands on her hips. "*Three* dates in a row?" She tilted her head and raised her eyebrows like she was asking for an explanation. One that Ashleigh couldn't give.

"What?" she asked to buy time.

With a quick shake of her head, Melanie laughed. "What do you mean 'what?' You know what. You don't hear word one from this guy for *six years*, but the moment he shows up and asks you out, you can't stay away from him?" She narrowed her eyes. "Do you really think that's a good idea?"

Of course it wasn't. It was the worst idea ever, but she couldn't tell her sister that. Not without drawing all kinds of questions. Instead, she shrugged. "He's only in town for a little while, so why not?"

Melanie made a scoffing sound. "Why not? I'll tell you why not. Because when he left six years ago, you pined after him for, I don't know," she crossed her arms over her chest, "forever?"

That was true. Painfully true.

Melanie dropped her arms to her sides and stared right into Ashleigh's eyes. "Look, I just don't want you to get hurt, okay?"

Ashleigh knew Melanie was sincere. Heaven knew Melanie had had her own share of hurt when it came to men, although she was happy now with Gage. But this was different. It was a business deal, kind of. "It will be fine," she said to reassure herself as much as her sister.

Melanie sighed and went back to decorating her Christmas cookies.

Glad the interrogation was over, Ashleigh fixed herself a snack, then went into her bedroom where she took out her laptop and pulled up the Bookmobile website. She browsed the options, getting more and more excited about getting a Bookmobile for the Emerald Falls Library. Until it hit her. She was profiting off of the death of Chase's mother. How despicable was she that she was getting excited over a material item when Chase was about to lose his only parent?

Guilt, dark and painful, pierced her to her core.

Accepting such an extravagant gift in exchange for granting a mother's dying wish wasn't right. Even if the Bookmobile wasn't for her personally, it was still something *she* wanted.

No. She couldn't do it. She couldn't accept it. If Emerald Falls were to get a Bookmobile, it would have to be through donations from legitimate donors. Not from Chase. Not in exchange for pretending to be engaged to him.

Though she was disappointed she wouldn't get some-thing that was so important to her, at the same time a feeling of peace settled over her. Simply doing this to be Sheila's Christmas Angel was the right decision. Besides, it was only for two months. She could do it for two months. Right?

CHAPTER 18

"You're not mad anymore, right?" Taylor asked Ashleigh on Monday morning as they sorted the books that had come in since the library had closed on Saturday evening.

Okay. Time to confess a little bit of the truth. If only to set the stage for her big engagement announcement in less than a week.

"No," Ashleigh said with a warm smile. "I'm not mad anymore."

Taylor exhaled a breath of relief. "Oh good. Because that guy was super-hot."

Shaking her head, Ashleigh laughed. "*That's* what makes it okay for you to throw me up on the auction block without warning and without my permission? Because he's hot?"

Which she totally agreed with. The hot part, not the okay part.

Looking at her like *Isn't it obvious?*, Taylor nodded. "Uh, yeah."

Setting the novel in her hands into the *Fiction* pile, Ashleigh turned to Taylor with a grimace. "There's something I need to tell you."

Taylor's eyes went wide. "No! You kissed him?"

That was the *last* thing she wanted to do. "Oh my goodness, no."

Taylor recoiled slightly. "Why would that be a bad thing? Or did you already forget how hot he is?"

That was something Ashleigh could never forget. "Because," she said with exaggerated flair, "Chase Matthews, the man who won the date, is my ex-boyfriend."

Taylor gasped so loudly that Ashleigh had to shush her. They were still in the library after all, and there were several patrons there.

"Sorry," Taylor whispered, her eyes glowing with shock. "But your *ex? Really?*" A smile slowly built on her lips. "Are you the one who broke up with him? I mean, he spent five grand to go on a date with you, so you must have broken his heart."

That was so far from reality that Ashleigh almost scoffed out loud. But she wasn't going to admit the truth either. Instead, she hedged. "It was a mutual decision." That was only true insofar as when Chase had told her he was leaving her and Emerald Falls behind, she hadn't thrown herself at him and begged him to stay, although that was only because she'd been so stunned by his announcement. Later on, before he'd left town, she'd come close to going to his house and begging him to stay, but when she'd remembered the determination she'd seen in his eyes, she'd known there was no changing his mind. Instead, she'd melted into a puddle of tears over and over until she had no tears left. Melanie had witnessed it all and had been there for her. It was no wonder Melanie was reticent about Ashleigh going out with Chase now.

What would Melanie say when Ashleigh told her they were engaged? She dreaded *that* particular conversation.

Taylor nodded like it all made sense. "Okay." Then that smile was back. "But he didn't *really* want to break up, did he?"

This conversation was over. "Can you finish this up? I have some other things I need to take care of."

Taylor nodded. "Sure."

Glad she didn't have to explain that horrendous chapter in her life, Ashleigh went to her desk and forced her mind to move away from Chase Matthews and the fact that she would be seeing him in a just a few hours and that in only a few days they would announce their engagement.

About to walk out the door for his date, Chase stopped when his mom said, "I'm so pleased that you and Ashleigh are going out again."

This was his chance to plant the seeds that would sell his mom on the idea that he and Ashleigh were really engaged. Of course, he wanted their announcement to be a surprise, but not an unbelievable one.

He sat beside his mom on the couch with a smile. "We're really hitting it off. I guess after all these years we've realized how much we missed each other."

Her expression soft, she tilted her head, "I can see how happy you are, Chase." She set her hand on his. "That makes me happy."

Okay. So far so good. Although he did feel guilty that he would be lying to his mom. But there was no other way to make her dying wish a reality. And he *had* discovered that he actually had missed Ashleigh, and he really *did* think they were hitting it off. At least on his side.

He stood. "Don't want to be late for my date."

His mom shook her head. "No, you do not."

Leaning down, he kissed her on the cheek. "I'll see you later."

When Chase pulled into Ashleigh's driveway at precisely seven o'clock, he was nervous. When he'd told her the day before that they needed to go out tonight, he'd gotten the impression that she wasn't eager to go on another date with him. Even so, she'd agreed and now he needed to make sure she had a good time.

The door on Chase's Lamborghini opened upward like a wing and he stepped out and closed it, then strode to Ashleigh's front door. Taking a moment to gather himself, he exhaled, then knocked.

CHAPTER 19

a knock sounded. Heart pounding with unexpected anticipation, Ashleigh walked toward the front door, but Avery reached it first, yanking it open. Still half a dozen steps away, Ashleigh stopped and watched as Chase's gaze fell to Avery. This gave her a chance to study him unobserved.

He wore dark jeans and a black leather jacket over a gray t-shirt. Taylor's comment about how hot he was filled Ashleigh's mind. He certainly was. *But,* she reminded herself, *he broke your heart. Don't ever forget that.*

"What's your name?" he was asking Avery.

"Avery," she said, her four-year-old voice filled with confidence.

Chase held out his hand and Avery took it, shaking it with a giggle.

"Is Ashleigh here?" he asked with a quick smile in Ashleigh's direction, which sent her heart tumbling around in her chest.

She had to shut those feelings right down. Everything he did was for show—they'd already agreed on that. She couldn't take a thing he did to heart.

"Aunt Ashy," Avery called out, "someone's here."

"Thanks, Avery," she said, taking the last few steps to the door while at the same time tamping down her growing attraction. She couldn't let her old feelings get the better of her. It would only bring her heartache.

She smiled at Chase, although her mouth felt tight, like she was forcing herself to be jovial. "Hi there."

"You look nice," he said with an appreciative grin.

"Thanks." She'd spent quite a bit of time picking out just the right outfit—a dark purple blouse that set off her blonde hair paired with form-fitting black jeans and heeled boots that added several inches to her five foot six inch height. "What do you have planned for us?"

His eyebrows slid together. "Wait. Don't we need to order something first?"

An image of the perfect Bookmobile flashed into her mind. "Not right now."

He tilted his head and narrowed his eyes. "Are you sure?"

"Yeah."

"Okay." He stepped back, allowing her to cross the threshold and walk onto the front porch.

She closed the door behind her, which was when she noticed the car in her driveway. The night was dark, but the lamps on either side of her garage cast enough light for her to see that Chase had driven a fancy black sports car. It looked expensive. If Chase could afford something like that, then buying a Bookmobile wouldn't be out of the question, would it? He'd said he could afford it.

When she reminded herself why she had decided to turn the Bookmobile down, she only felt a small twinge of regret at her decision—one she had yet to share with Chase, but one that she was going to stick to. If only for her own peace of mind. She had to do this fake engagement thing for the right reason. Not for profit, but out of compassion.

"Nice ride," she said.

Chase laughed. "Jordyn thinks so too, which is why she suggested we trade for the day yesterday."

"And here I had the impression she was just being a thoughtful sister."

That made Chase laugh harder. He touched a spot on the passenger door, and it swung upward.

Kind of impressed, Ashleigh glanced into the interior before turning to Chase. "It's not going to take off, is it?"

He grinned. "If I go fast enough, it'll just feel like we're flying."

She laughed and slid inside. Moments later, Chase got behind the wheel.

They chatted comfortably, and when they walked into a

restaurant with a karaoke stage, she couldn't hold back a giggle. This was something she'd always wanted to do but had never been brave enough to try. "Karaoke?"

"Back in the day you said you wanted to try it," Chase said with a grin.

Ignoring the reference to their past, she said, "I want to sing Christmas songs."

"Ha! I knew you would." Crinkles formed around his eyes as he smiled.

Soon they were seated right up front where someone was already on stage singing.

"It'll be easier to get on stage from here," Chase said in a low voice.

Not able to hold back a smile, Ashleigh secretly admitted that she was glad she'd agreed to this date. Maybe it wouldn't be so bad once they were fake-engaged to hang out with Chase. As long as they kept it platonic.

When they were done eating, Chase raised his eyebrows. "You ready to get up there?"

"Only if you join me." If she was going to make a fool of herself, he would have to be by her side.

He pushed his chair back. "Let's do it."

No one was singing at that moment, and when they reached the edge of the stage, the employee who was in charge of the karaoke machine asked what song they wanted to sing.

"We want to sing a Christmas song," Ashleigh said. "Together."

The music man smiled. "I have the perfect choice."

Trusting him, Ashleigh climbed onto the stage with Chase right behind her. Moments later the music started and the words appeared on a screen in front of them. Ashleigh immediately recognized the song *Baby, It's Cold Outside*. She'd always liked that song, but singing it with Chase would be a little different since it was about a couple who spent the evening together and when it was time to say goodnight, the man wanted to still spend time with the woman but she kept saying she needed to go, but the man kept trying to convince her to stay.

Too bad Chase hadn't felt that way when he'd chosen to leave her and Emerald Falls.

Pushing aside any hard feelings, Ashleigh focused on the screen, and with everyone in the restaurant watching, she started singing and Chase chimed right in with his part.

As they sang, Ashleigh couldn't help but think how much the song mirrored the conversation she and Chase had had the day before when Chase had convinced her to be fake-engaged to him even though she'd resisted it.

They sang through all the verses and Ashleigh really enjoyed herself. When the song finished no one was waiting to go on, so they told the music man that they wanted to continue.

A few moments later a new song began—*The Twelve Days of Christmas*.

She sang the first verse.

On the first day of Christmas

My true love gave to me
A partridge in a pear tree

As she sang the phrase *true love*, she couldn't help but wonder if she would ever find her true love. When she'd been twenty, she'd believed that Chase was her true love. Now though, she knew that had been just a fantasy. One that he didn't share.

Chase sang the next verse.

On the second day of Christmas
My true love gave to me
Two turtle doves
And a partridge in a pear tree

His voice was silky smooth, and as she imagined what it would feel like to have him hold her in his arms and tell her that she was his true love, longing thrummed through her. She had to keep her emotions in check, had to remind herself that they were only doing this for show in preparation for announcing their fake engagement.

They continued taking turns with each verse, gazing at each other as they sang. That's when it hit Ashleigh that of all the women Chase knew, he'd chosen *her* to help his mother's dying wish come true. Breathless at the realization, she was overwhelmed with a whole mix of emotions, and without even thinking about it, she slid her hand into his, which earned her a look of surprise.

With his hand clasped in hers, he sang the final verse. The song ended and the crowd burst into applause. Suddenly remembering they were standing in front of a bunch of strangers, Ashleigh felt very self-conscious. Extricating her hand from Chase's, she made her way down the steps and back to their table.

CHAPTER 20

*C*hase watched Ashleigh as she glided off of the stage and back to their table. All kinds of unexpected emotions welled up inside him—until he remembered that they were putting on a show to convince everyone that they were on the cusp of getting engaged. He knew if he was in the audience, he would be convinced. Maybe they should move up their timeline.

Striding down the steps and off of the stage, he made his way back to the table where Ashleigh was focused on digging through her purse.

"That was fun," he said as he slid into the seat across from her.

She looked up at him, her expression guarded. "Uh-huh." Then she shifted her eyes to her drink before lifting the glass and taking a sip.

Why did it feel like she was avoiding looking at him?

"We need to talk about the Bookmobile," he said to force her attention.

Her eyes shot to his face. "What about it?"

What was going on? The day before she'd *insisted* that he order the Bookmobile right away—made it a stipulation of their deal, in fact. But now she seemed uninterested. Why?

Then it hit him. She was going to back out of their deal.

Panic, powerful and swift, washed over him. What would he do if she changed her mind?

He had to prevent her from backing out of it.

He pulled his phone out of his pocket. "What's the website? I can order it right now."

Her eyebrows tugged together and her lips pursed. "I don't want you to buy a Bookmobile, Chase."

Oh no. Here it comes.

He set his phone on the table. "But that was part of our agreement."

Her expression was pained as she sighed heavily. "I know. But I changed my mind."

"You can't do that."

Her head tilted slightly as a look of annoyance splashed across her face. "Yes I can. I can do whatever I want."

Oh boy. And the trouble was, she was right. If she didn't want to go through with this fake engagement, he couldn't make her. But maybe he could change her mind. Glad he'd gone shopping that day, he smiled. "Let's go somewhere quieter so we can talk."

She nodded like she wanted to do the same thing.

Together they stood and moved to a booth in the back corner of the room where they could have a conversation that didn't involve speaking in loud voices. She slid into the booth first and he sat right beside her.

Rather surprised that Chase was sitting so close to her, Ashleigh was also wary. Having him *right there* was a bit disconcerting. Especially after the strong emotions she'd felt while they'd been singing. She had to get a grip on herself or this fake engagement would spiral out of control. At least for her. The risk of heartbreak was growing with each day she spent with him.

"I have something for you," Chase said, then he reached into his pocket and pulled out a tiny velvet box.

Oh my gosh! Is he doing this already?

Stunned at how fast this was happening, Ashleigh only calmed when she reminded herself it was all an act, all pretend. Good thing she'd managed to gather herself because he was sitting so close to her that if she'd let herself think it was real she might have done something she would later regret, like kiss him. Instead, she coolly asked, "What's that?"

He smiled. "I guess we can call it a prop." Then he opened the lid. A huge princess cut diamond ring was nestled inside.

Ashleigh couldn't stop a gasp from escaping her lips. She lifted her eyes to his. "It's not real though, right?"

A wide smile curved his lips as his eyes twinkled. "Oh no. It's very real."

Her mouth snapped closed and her eyes went wide. "I can't wear that."

His smile melted away. "Please don't back out, Ashleigh. I really need you to do this."

Back out? Why did he think she was backing out? She was just worried about losing the ring that had to be worth more than she earned in a year.

He had to convince Ashleigh to follow through. His mom had been so serene and happy when he'd told her how well things were going with Ashleigh that he couldn't bear the thought of telling her it was already over.

"I'm not backing out," she said, her eyes narrowing in obvious confusion. "Why would you think that?"

Relief swelled inside him. Wait, if she wasn't backing out, then why wouldn't she wear the ring and why didn't she want the Bookmobile? Ready to get some answers without making assumptions, he smiled. "Okay, why can't you wear this ring?"

She shook her head like *Isn't it obvious?* "Because it's too expensive. I mean, what if I lose it?"

He laughed. Was that all? "You're not going to lose it. But even if you did, it's insured."

"Oh."

He took the ring out of the box. "Now, will you wear it?"

"I thought we were waiting until Friday."

He shrugged. "Why wait? I mean, after that performance on stage it won't come as a great surprise to anyone who was watching that we're in love."

She bit her lip. "I suppose so. Although no one we know was watching."

"True." He took her hand and uncurled her fingers so that her palm was open, then he set the ring in her hand. "Tell you what. You take the ring and put it on when you feel ready. As long as it's no later than Friday."

She stared at the ring in her palm for a moment, then she lifted those blue eyes to his, which tugged at his heart. Memories of all the times he'd stared into those eyes swept over him, ending with the last time and all the confusion and hurt he'd seen there when he'd announced his decision to leave Emerald Falls.

Guilt pierced him, but he blinked it away. The past was the past and now was now. Besides, this was a simple business arrangement. Which reminded him... He curled her fingers over the ring and released her hand. "What about that Bookmobile? Why don't you want me to buy it?" He squinted at her. "Do you want to wait so that it won't be obvious it's tied to our engagement?" That made sense, now that he thought about it.

She shook her head. "No. I don't want it anymore."

He could see in her eyes that that wasn't true. She wanted

it badly and saying otherwise made her flinch. So, what was the deal? "Why not?"

She shook her head. "It just...it doesn't seem right for me to get something so extravagant when your mom is...well, when she's dying."

Deeply moved, he had the urge to pull her into his arms, but he wasn't sure if that would break her touching rule, so he kept his hands to himself. "That means a lot to me." And it showed him how truly selfless she could be. There was literally nothing in this for her, yet she was willing to sacrifice two months of her life to make his mom happy.

His heart swelled with gratitude toward her. She was an amazing woman. Had he made an irreversible error in breaking up with her? But no, nothing was irreversible, right?

"I need to make one thing clear," she said, her face stern.

"What?"

"We've got to keep this thing strictly platonic, Chase."

With her unyielding expression, he said the only thing he could. "Of course. I was thinking the same thing."

She nodded. "Good. I'm glad we're on the same page." Then she slipped the ring onto her left ring finger as she smiled at him. "Looks like we're engaged."

For some reason, this moment wasn't as exciting and romantic as Chase had thought it would be.

CHAPTER 21

*N*ow that she and Chase had made it official, Ashleigh had to prepare herself to break the news to her friends and family.

"We should have a dinner to announce this," Chase said.

"No. No no no." She waved her arms like she was warding off a spell. "I can't face all of those people at once and lie to them." She sighed. "I have to do it one at a time."

She knew how ridiculous that sounded. How could she lie to those she loved? But it was for a good cause. And it was only temporary. When the truth came out, they would understand. Especially after Sheila...well, after the cancer won. No one would be able to blame her for wanting to grant Sheila the one thing she wanted more than anything else in the world.

"Wouldn't you rather get it over with all at the same time?" Chase asked.

"Not really."

He nodded. "Okay." Then he smiled. "My mom's gonna freak."

She laughed. "Hopefully in a good way."

He grinned. "Oh, yeah. It'll be awesome." He paused. "We'll take my mom and Jordyn to dinner to tell them."

"When do you want to do that?"

"Tomorrow?"

Man, this was moving fast, but that was the idea, wasn't it? "Okay." On the outside she was calm, but inside she was having her own freak-out. That, and a sudden bout of guilt. Because everyone would be so happy for her, but it would all be a lie.

"When are you going tell your sister?" Chase asked.

Oh man. When she pictured *that* particular conversation, dread nearly swamped her. Melanie would have all kinds of questions and would most certainly have doubts. And she would warn her about rushing into something. Ahhh! She didn't want to think about it. "Before going to dinner tomorrow, I guess."

He must have been able to tell she was stressed over it, because he gazed steadily at her with those green eyes that she'd always been drawn to and said in a soft voice, "I won't say anything to anyone until you give me the word, okay? That will give you time to tell your sister and whoever else you need to tell."

Why did he have to be so sweet? But he always had been —up until the moment he'd broken her heart. "Thanks, Chase. I'll let you know when I've told her."

His eyes sparkled as he smiled. "Just don't wait too long. That dinner is tomorrow."

Thanks for the reminder. "I promise I'll do it soon."

He nodded. "You ready to head home?"

Where she couldn't avoid Melanie? Then again, she didn't have to tell her the moment she saw her. Although if this was a real engagement she would want to shout it from the rooftops, right? She needed to get her head in the game. "Yes, let's go."

When they reached her house, Chase walked her to the door. She turned to him with a smile. "Thanks for the fun night. Karaoke was a blast."

"We'll have to do it again."

The promise of more time with him sent a small swarm of butterflies swooping around in her belly. The butterflies needed to chill because she and Chase were fake-engaged. Of course the two of them would spend time together. At least for the next two months. Besides, they were keeping it platonic. They had to.

She nodded. "Good night."

"Good night." He turned and strode back to his Lamborghini, then climbed inside, driving off a moment later.

Bracing herself for a conversation with Melanie, Ashleigh opened the front door and went in.

No one was in the living room and the only light came from the Christmas tree. Red, green, blue, and yellow lights flickered on and off, on and off, casting a festive glow into the small space. Ashleigh wandered over to the tree and stood in front of it, then ran her fingers over the soft pine needles as she inhaled the wonderful scent coming from the fresh tree.

"You're back," Melanie said from behind her.

Ashleigh spun around, hiding her left hand behind her. "Yes."

Glancing down the hall, Melanie said, "I just put Avery to bed." Then she narrowed her eyes. "What's going on?"

Was she so easy to read? "What do you mean?"

Melanie tilted her head and narrowed her eyes. "Something's up, Ash. I can tell." Then she straightened, her expression disapproving. "Did you agree to *another* date with Chase?"

Well, they hadn't set a date, just gotten engaged. The whole fake engagement idea seemed utterly ridiculous now that she had to tell Melanie about it and Ashleigh nearly choked on a hysterical laugh. Instead, she managed to keep herself under control, shaking her head. "Actually, no, we didn't schedule a date." Guess they'd been too busy talking about their engagement.

Melanie huffed out a sigh. "Good. I'm glad you're getting past this ridiculous phase of dating *him*."

Oh boy. Maybe she should wait to tell her their big news.

Melanie's eyes narrowed again as she stared at Ashleigh's

left arm, which was still behind her back. Without warning, she grabbed Ashleigh's wrist and yanked her hand forward, revealing the mammoth engagement ring.

A loud gasp burst from Melanie's mouth as she stared at Ashleigh's finger. Lifting Ashleigh's hand, Melanie pointed to the ring. "What is *this*?!" She lifted her accusing eyes from the ring to Ashleigh's face.

Not liking the tone of her sister's voice, Ashleigh felt defensive. She didn't have to get anyone's permission to live her life. "It's a ring, Mel."

She dropped Ashleigh's hand. "I can see that. Did Chase give it to you?"

"Yes."

"*Why* did he give it to you?"

This wasn't how she'd seen this conversation going. To be honest, she hadn't seen it going well, but this was a lot worse than even she'd pictured. "We're engaged."

Melanie closed her eyes and slowly shook her head, then her eyes snapped open. "What on earth is happening?"

She wished she could tell her the truth, but she'd promised she wouldn't tell anyone. What if Sheila found out it was all make-believe? It would destroy her happiness and she would die feeling even worse.

"Chase and I are engaged." She desperately hoped Melanie would accept reality—well, fake-reality—and stop giving her a hard time.

"I don't believe this."

Was her acting that bad? Was she so unconvincing?

Melanie threw her hands up. "I can't believe you fell for that man again. After the way he crushed your heart."

Okay, so she *did* believe her. She just didn't approve. No surprise there. Time to get into her role as ecstatic fiancée.

"I love him, Mel, okay? And he loves me. We love each other." They'd literally never said those words to each other. Even when they'd dated for that year. She had been in love with him, but she'd never told him, and he'd never told her that he felt that way. At the time, to her, it had been unspoken, but now she knew that she could never assume anything. Not when it came to Chase.

Melanie was staring at her like she'd grown a second head. "It's just...it's so sudden." She squinted. "Are you sure you want to do this?"

She wasn't sure about anything anymore. "Yeah."

Melanie stared at her a moment longer like she was waiting to see if Ashleigh meant it. Then she sighed. "When is this wedding going to be?"

Wedding? Holy cow, that sounded serious. Then again, engagements led to weddings so the question wasn't unreasonable.

"Uh, we haven't gotten that far."

"Good. Maybe you'll come to your senses before you plan anything concrete."

Okay. This was getting ridiculous. What if she really *was* engaged? Melanie wasn't showing any support at all.

"You know, you could be happy for me."

Melanie's lips clamped shut as she stared at her, then her

eyes softened. "I'm sorry, Ash. I guess I just need time to get used to the idea that you're engaged to Chase Matthews."

That made two of them.

Shortly after getting home from dropping Ashleigh off, Chase heard his phone chime a text. It was from Ashleigh. *I told Melanie.*

Rather surprised that she'd already told her sister, when he read the cryptic message, Chase couldn't help but wonder how it had gone. Ashleigh hadn't seemed overly excited to give her sister the news. He didn't know Melanie very well, but he had to assume she was aware that Ashleigh had been hurt when he'd left. That couldn't put him very high on Melanie's list of favorite people.

He sent a reply. *What did she say?*

Minutes later, she replied. *She bought it.*

Hmm. That didn't give him any idea how it had gone, but if Melanie, the person who knew Ashleigh best, believed her, then everyone would. And why did her phrasing of *She bought it* rub him the wrong way? After all, it *was* all a ruse. Buying it was exactly what they needed people to do.

Pushing aside his unexpected reaction, he thought about his mom and how thrilled she would be to hear the news. She'd already gone to bed—she seemed to be getting more tired by the day—but he would tell her when he took her to dinner the next night.

CHAPTER 22

The next morning Chase was up before the sun, but that didn't mean he was the first one up.

"Good morning," Jordyn said with a bright smile when he wandered into the kitchen.

How was it that his sister was always so cheerful when the sun hadn't even risen yet?

Ready for a run, he wore sweatpants and a hoodie. "Hey."

Jordyn was sitting at the table downing a plate of scrambled eggs and toast.

"Mom still asleep?" he asked as he grabbed a protein drink from the fridge.

Worry washed across Jordyn's face. "Yeah. And she went to bed early last night."

It felt strange to not have his mom with them at breakfast. All throughout his growing up years she had been a fixture at breakfast, making sure he and Jordyn got a good start to their day.

"What time does the nurse come?" he asked. Thinking about their reality, the one where a nurse had to come over several times a week to help his mom, made a knot form in his throat. She might not even be up to going out to dinner.

"She'll be here in about an hour." Jordyn blinked several times like she was trying to keep tears at bay.

Seeing his stoic sister getting emotional tore at his heart. Tears sprang into his eyes. Clearing his throat to cover his emotions, he nodded.

She smiled softly. "I'm glad you're here, Chase."

"Me too." He couldn't imagine *not* being there when his mom needed him the most. As successful as he was, all the money in the world couldn't cure her when cancer had infiltrated her body. Trying not to visualize what the world would look like with his mom not in it, he changed the subject. "What are your plans today?"

The shift in topic seemed to help Jordyn too. A bright smile lit her face. "The usual. Go to my gorgeous studio and paint."

He smiled in return, beyond pleased that the studio he'd had built for her in the backyard served her so well and made her so happy. "Sounds like a good plan."

She stood from the table and gave him a hug. "You are the best brother."

He hugged her back, affection for his sister washing over him. Pretty soon it would just be the two of them. He was just grateful that they had always been close and that they could truly rely on each other.

"You're not too bad yourself," he said with a chuckle.

She stepped away and smiled at him. "What are *your* plans?"

"Go for a run and then work all day."

"Borrrriiiing," she trilled.

He laughed. "Just like painting doesn't seem like work to you, what I do doesn't seem like work to me." He cocked his head. "Well, maybe sometimes it does."

"I love to paint, but sometimes it feels like work to me too. Like, when a piece doesn't come out the way I'd seen it in my head and I have to work hard to fix it." She smiled. "Still, I'm a very lucky girl to be able to do what I love for a living."

"A living, huh?"

This won him a laugh, because though she earned a small income from her work, if it wasn't for the money he gave her, she would have to work a regular job. "Eventually I'll be richer than you, bro."

He hoped that was true because he loved her work and he was glad he was able to support her so that she could do what she was passionate about. "I'm sure you will be."

With that, he headed out the door, and as he ran, his thoughts turned to Ashleigh. How was she feeling that morning about their engagement? Would it be awkward for her to tell people? Would they give her a hard time for jumping into an engagement with him?

Then he thought about her decision to not order the Bookmobile even though she clearly wanted it so badly. She was doing this for all the right reasons.

Powerful emotions toward her welled up inside him and he wished she was with him at that very moment. But what if she was? What would he do? She'd made it explicitly clear that their relationship was to remain platonic. Would she at least allow him to give her a hug? Friends hugged.

Silently laughing at himself, he focused on his run, and when he got home he found his mom up and about and Jordyn gone.

"Well, good morning," his mom said, cheerful as ever, although she looked drawn and tired.

Remembering his earlier thoughts about what the world would be like without her, he swallowed down his sadness and smiled brightly. "Good morning."

She looked him over. "You're sure dedicated, running on a cold December morning."

He laughed. "It's not like we live where it snows."

"Thank goodness for that."

He wanted to blurt out his news then and there, just to see her reaction, but it would be better to do it in style. Even if he had to have a meal brought in. He would let her decide what she wanted to do. "I'd love to take you to dinner this evening. If you're up to it. Or I can have something brought in."

"I'd love to go out."

"Great. I'll see if Jordyn can come too."

"That would be lovely."

He visited with her until the nurse came, then he kissed her on the cheek and went into his room where he sent Ashleigh a text. *Scheduled dinner tonight with Mom and J. Meet us there?*

Ashleigh replied a short time later. *Ok.*

Her one-word answer told him volumes. She wasn't thrilled about this, but at least she had agreed to it. He told her where and when, then he sent Jordyn a text and invited her to join them. She agreed.

When he and his mom arrived at The Glasshouse that evening, she hooked her arm through his as they walked in together. Once they were seated, Chase studied her. She looked better than she had that morning—her color was good and the bags under her eyes were diminished. Then again, she was good at using makeup.

"How are you feeling?" he asked as she took a sip of her water.

"Oh, you know. Not bad."

Not bad wasn't the same as good. "Is there anything I can do for you?"

She smiled softly. "Having you here in Emerald Falls is the best medicine."

He was glad his being there could make such a difference. "I'm glad I could come."

Jordyn arrived a few moments later, joining them at the table. "Now the party can begin," she said with a smirk as she slid into her seat.

He hadn't told them that Ashleigh would be coming—he wanted it to be a surprise. But as he imagined their expressions when he and Ashleigh broke their news, he couldn't hold back a smile.

"What are you grinning about?" Jordyn asked.

Just then Ashleigh walked into the restaurant. She hadn't seen him yet, but at the sight of her, his heart did a little flip that caught him by surprise. She was just as beautiful as she'd always been, and knowing she was *his*, at least for the next two months, did funny things to his insides. Of course, it was all pretend, but no one else knew that, and for the duration of their charade, he would have her all to himself.

He caught her eye and motioned her over. His mom and Jordyn looked to see who he was communicating with. Keeping his focus on Ashleigh, Chase ignored the curious looks on their faces.

"Hello," Ashleigh said when she reached their table. She wore black slacks that flattered her slim figure and a red sweater that complemented her blonde hair and blue eyes.

Chase stood and almost took her into his arms. Until he remembered their agreement. No touching, except an occasional hand-hold. "Thank you for joining us."

"Of course." She turned her attention to his mom. "Hello, Sheila. It's so good to see you." Ashleigh bent to give his mom a hug.

Chase desperately wished she would give *him* a hug. Swallowing down his unexpected desire, Chase noticed the engagement ring was absent from her finger. He assumed it was to keep their secret until he was ready to tell his family.

"Hi, Jordyn," Ashleigh said with a smile at his sister.

"Hi." Jordyn glanced at Chase with a wrinkled brow.

Chase held out a chair for Ashleigh, which she gracefully slid into.

"This is a surprise," Shelia said. "A very nice surprise."

Thankfully, the server came, distracting everyone for a moment. They placed their orders, and then Chase's mom looked between him and Ashleigh. "Okay, you two. What's going on?"

Ashleigh looked at him with raised eyebrows as if to say, *Let's tell them now.*

Nodding imperceptibly, he looked between his mom and Jordyn. "We have something to tell you."

His mom gasped as her eyes widened. "No."

He laughed. "We haven't told you anything yet."

Chuckling, she said, "I can see it though. It's written all over both of your faces."

"Okay," he said with a grin. "Tell us. What's our news?"

"Obviously, you're back together."

It was so much more and so much less than that, all at the same time. "You're getting warm."

Jordyn's lips pursed. "Just tell us."

He took Ashleigh's hand—she couldn't object to him doing that at this moment—and smiled. "We're engaged."

His mom's gasp was even louder this time. "What?"

Jordyn, he noticed, narrowed her eyes like she didn't

believe it. She'd always been very perceptive. Deciding to focus on his mom, he smiled. "Surprise."

Looking like she totally bought it—and was delighted—his mom asked, "When did this happen?"

The pure joy on her face made the deceit worth it, although Chase still felt a surge of guilt. Wondering how Ashleigh felt, he glanced her way.

CHAPTER 23

*a*shleigh felt slightly sick inside. Lying wasn't something she was comfortable with, and this was no exception. If it wasn't for the elation on Sheila's face, she would probably confess the truth. And when she looked at Jordyn, who seemed more skeptical than joyful, she shifted uncomfortably in her chair.

"When *did* this happen, Chase?" Jordyn asked. "I mean, you guys have only been on a few dates."

"I know it's sudden," Chase said, which made Ashleigh glad because she didn't want to be the one to explain, "but can't you just be happy for us? Like Mom is?"

Jordyn glanced at Sheila and apparently noticed her mom's jubilation, because she quietly sighed and smiled in a way that Ashleigh could tell was forced, which begged the question, Why was Jordyn so dubious?

Christmas music played in the background and bright red poinsettias were placed throughout the space, creating a festive mood and reminding Ashleigh that this was the time of year to create happy memories—memories that Chase and Jordyn would especially need in years to come.

On impulse, she leaned toward Chase and kissed him on the cheek.

He turned to her with obvious surprise.

Come on, Chase. You're going to give this away before we've even started. Even as she thought it, she acknowledged that she'd broken her own rule that they not touch, so who could blame him for being thrown off?

"Where's the ring?" Jordyn asked. Her tone wasn't exactly a challenge, but it wasn't happiness and light either.

Ashleigh gently pulled her hand from Chase's and picked up her purse from the floor. She dug around until she found the ring, then slid it onto her left ring finger and held out her hand for inspection.

Jordyn's eyebrows shot up and she looked at Chase with approval. "Nice." Then she smiled at Ashleigh. "Congratulations."

She seemed sincere, although Ashleigh didn't know her well enough to know for sure. In any case, the fact that this was all pretend sent guilt slicing through her again.

You're Sheila's Christmas Angel, she reminded herself. *Just keep that in mind.*

"Yes," Sheila said with tears in her eyes, her gaze going

between Ashleigh and Chase. "Congratulations." Then she looked right at Ashleigh. "You have no idea how happy this makes me."

Actually, she did, but Sheila's frank admission was like a salve on her soul where the guilt had left a deep cut. Serenity slid over her, allowing her to smile with sincerity.

"When," Sheila began before hesitating, "when will the wedding be?" A tentative smile lifted her lips. "I mean, I'd... I'd sure like to...to be there for it."

Oh my goodness. Could this be any sadder?

The server set their food on the table, giving everyone a moment to settle. Ashleigh took the opportunity to look at Chase for guidance. They hadn't discussed what to do in a situation like this.

He smiled at her in what she assumed was supposed to be a reassuring look, but she could read the panic in his eyes.

"Uh," he said as he straightened the napkin on his lap and faced his mother, "we haven't set a date yet."

Sheila looked from Chase to Ashleigh and back again. "I...I don't want to push you, but maybe you can do it soon. I mean, why wait, right?"

Holy crap! This wasn't part of the plan.

Alarm wound its way up Ashleigh's throat, making her want to shout that this was all pretend. She wasn't about to marry Chase. Not for real. Not when he didn't love her. Not when he'd left her because she meant nothing to him.

He glanced at her, clearly forcing a smile. "We'll have to

talk about it." Then he turned to his mother. "But I'm sure we can work something out."

What?! Work something out? What was he talking about? There was nothing to work out. Only a fake engagement that would eventually end.

Sheila's eyes lit up. "A Christmas wedding. That would be amazing." Her eyes closed in what looked like ecstasy, then she opened them and smiled. "Oh! That would be so lovely."

Panic gripped Ashleigh and she felt the blood drain from her face. Jordyn was looking at her with suspicion again. Then it hit her. Jordyn must think Ashleigh was after her brother's money. Ashleigh didn't know how much he had, but he was obviously wealthy. If only Jordyn knew how wrong she was.

One problem at a time. Then again, all of her problems stemmed from the same thing—pretending to be engaged.

Ashleigh shoved a smile onto her lips and turned to Chase.

His eyes broadcast S.O.S. as he asked, "What do you think, sweetheart?"

He wanted *her* to fix it? Come on! "What do I think about what?" she asked sweetly.

"About getting married on Christmas?"

"I don't…that is…I'm not sure that would give us enough time to plan."

Chase's expression relaxed slightly. He turned to his mom. "That's true."

Sheila's expression fell, making Ashleigh wish she could

enthusiastically jump on board the Christmas Wedding Train.

Jordyn snorted a laugh. "With all of your money you could pull it together as fast as you want to."

Kind of annoyed with Chase because she was only in this position due to his crazy scheme, she wanted to see him squirm. She turned to him with a smile. "That's true."

His eyes went wide and his mouth fell open. "It is?"

Suppressing a laugh, Ashleigh nodded. "Mmm-hmm."

"Is that what you want?"

Definitely not, and it was up to him to fix this. Ashleigh looked at the undisguised hope in Shelia's eyes, then at Jordyn with her raised eyebrows, before turning back to Chase. "I want whatever you want, sweetheart." There. That certainly made it clear that it was his responsibility to put things back in order.

Chase's eyes were tight, but he smiled gamely. "Okay. All right." His smile grew as he turned to his mom. "Let's do it. A Christmas Wedding."

Tears filled Sheila's eyes as she exhaled softly. "Oh."

Wait, what?! Chase was supposed to make an excuse of why it wouldn't work, not lock it in.

She kicked him under the table.

"Ow." He looked at her with a frown.

Ashleigh stood. "Excuse me. I need to use the ladies' room." What she really wanted was to speak to Chase in private so she could throttle him without witnesses. Instead, she'd take a moment to gather herself.

Ever the one with gracious manners, Chase stood, his expression strained.

Ignoring him, Ashleigh turned and strode to the ladies' room. Standing in front of the mirror, Ashleigh had barely had a moment to take a breath when the door pushed open and Jordyn burst into the room

CHAPTER 24

"What is going on?" Jordyn asked as she stomped over to Ashleigh, capturing her gaze in the mirror.

Did Jordyn see through everything and know this was fake, or did she think it was something else entirely? "What do you mean?"

Jordyn turned away from the mirror and faced Ashleigh, so Ashleigh did the same, meeting Jordyn's angry glare.

"You're taking advantage of my brother."

A loud scoffing sound shot out of Ashleigh's mouth before she could stop it. It had been an instinctual response, but one she now regretted, based on the anger flashing in Jordyn's eyes.

"How dare you," Jordyn said, her voice low and laced with fury. "How dare you get Chase to *propose marriage*," she nearly spit the words out, "when he's so emotionally vulnerable."

Oh, how Ashleigh wished she could set Jordyn straight, but that would ruin the whole plan. Instead, she played dumb. "What are you talking about?"

Jordyn huffed out a sigh. "You're kidding, right? I mean, I'm sure you're aware that my mother is terminally ill. That's why Chase is in town, after all."

"Yeah, he told me."

She nodded like she'd already figured that out. "Just because he spent five grand to go out with you doesn't mean he wants to spend the rest of his life with you."

That stung. Deeply. But only because Ashleigh already knew it was true. She didn't need to be told by Chase's protective younger sister. Hurt and humiliated, Ashleigh spoke without thinking. "It was his idea to get engaged, not mine." Uh-oh. Had she said too much?

The truth of the matter seemed to sail right over Jordyn's head. "You could have said no."

Yes, and she had. At first. Until Chase had agreed to buy the Bookmobile. That had bought her agreement. So, apparently his money did matter to her. Fresh guilt swept over her, until she reminded herself that she'd turned down the Bookmobile and was now doing this for purely altruistic reasons, although after everything that had happened at dinner and with the accusations flying from Jordyn, she was ready to call the whole thing off.

Not wanting to have hard feelings between her and Jordyn, but also not about to let herself be bullied, Ashleigh said, "I understand your concern, but this is between Chase and me."

Jordyn pursed her lips, then shook her head before storming out of the bathroom.

That went well. Ashleigh turned back to the mirror, but as she reached up to fix her hair she noticed her hands were shaking. She hated confrontations, but she'd already been on edge, so it hadn't taken much to push her far enough to speak her mind. She just hoped Jordyn didn't hate her now. Because she hadn't done anything wrong. All she was trying to do was bring a smile to Sheila's face.

Sighing dramatically, Ashleigh took one last moment to gather herself before she walked back to the table. Only Chase and Sheila were there.

"Where's Jordyn?" Ashleigh asked Chase.

"She said she didn't feel well, so she went home." Chase gave her a look that said he knew something had happened in the bathroom but he would ask for the details later.

"Oh."

Glad she wouldn't have to face Chase's sister during the rest of the meal, Ashleigh focused on slicing off a small piece of chicken.

"I know just the place you can have your wedding," Sheila said, her voice having lost none of its enthusiasm from earlier.

Ashleigh glanced at Chase in the hopes he would nip this

in the bud, but he looked completely serene. Was he okay with this? How could he be?

Maybe it would have been better if Jordyn was there to speak her mind and put a stop to this. Since she wasn't, it was up to Ashleigh.

"You know," she started, bracing herself for the look of disappointment that was sure to come, "as wonderful as a Christmas wedding would be, I'm just not sure that it will work."

Haunting sadness, not disappointment, filled Sheila's eyes. "Oh. I see."

Sheila wasn't going to argue this. A mix of crushing guilt and tremendous relief rolled over Ashleigh.

"Don't be silly, sweetheart," Chase said as he put an arm around her shoulders, "we'll *make* it work."

Ashleigh snapped her head in his direction. What was he *talking* about? Realizing her mouth was hanging open in an unflattering manner, she clamped it shut. As a bonus, it kept her from saying something she would regret, like, *Have you lost your freaking mind or have you just forgotten this is fake?*

"How," she managed to ask, "will we make it work?"

Looking perfectly calm and composed, he smiled. "I'll explain the details to you later."

Oh. He had a plan. That was good news. For a minute there she'd thought he'd let the thought of disappointing his mother replace his common sense.

Not feeling a whole lot better, but knowing there was nothing she could do for the moment, Ashleigh ate her chicken and listened to Sheila talk about the venue she had in mind.

When the meal was mercifully over and many of the plans had been discussed, Ashleigh told Sheila goodbye before Chase walked her to her car.

"I'll come over to your house after I take my mom home so we can talk more about this," he said as they stood next to her car.

"Melanie will be there, so that won't work." That was all she needed—to have Melanie overhear any of their conversation, or to have Melanie confront Chase about the way he'd left Ashleigh six years earlier and had now proposed marriage.

"Okay. I'll pick you up and we'll go somewhere we can talk in private."

As long as they straightened out this mess, that was fine with her. "All right."

He opened the driver's door for her and she slid inside, and after he closed her door, she drove home, eager to hear what he had in mind.

CHAPTER 25

*C*hase didn't know if Ashleigh was going to go for his idea, but it was the only solution, and as he parked his Lamborghini in her driveway, he rehearsed in his mind the way he would sell it.

She stepped onto the porch before he had a chance to get out of his car. Surprised, he opened his door and climbed out, but she walked toward him before he could get to her.

Eager much? But of course she was. She had to be dying inside to know how they were going to pull this off.

"Hi, there," he said with a confident smile. At least it felt confident, but at the look on her face—like he was nuts—his smile faded.

"Hi." She stopped in front of him, her face broadcasting anxiety. "Let's go for a drive."

"Okay." He helped her into his car and off they went.

They were both quiet as he drove. Chase wondered what she was thinking, although he had a pretty good idea. Moments later she told him what was on her mind.

"Why did you tell your mom we would get married on Christmas? Have you lost your mind? That's two weeks from *tomorrow*." She audibly sighed. "I mean, we weren't supposed to get past the engagement."

Glad he'd come up with a solution, he turned to her with a smile. "No, I haven't lost my mind. And I have an idea."

She crossed her arms over her chest and started at him hard. "I'm all ears."

Pushing a confident smile onto his lips, he said, "We'll hold the wedding, but it won't be real."

Her head jerked back as her arms fell to her sides. "What?"

"Hear me out."

Her lips compressed and she folded her arms again, her eyes like laser beams boring into his skull, like she was trying to melt the harebrained idea right out of his head.

"I'll hire an actor to perform the marriage," he said, eager to get her approval, although he wouldn't be surprised if she chose to end the entire charade instead. "So, it will *look like* we got married, but we won't actually *be* married."

"*That's* your brilliant idea? To trick all of our family and friends into thinking we got married when we really didn't?" She shook her head. "Do you know how upset everyone will be when the truth comes out?"

He hadn't thought that far ahead. His only concern had

been for his mom and trying desperately to make her happy before the cancer took her. "I take it you don't like my idea."

Actually, Ashleigh had to give him credit. The idea wasn't without merit. Still, she wasn't prepared to agree that easily.

"Your sister hates me," she said instead.

Now it was Chase's turn to be shocked. "What are you talking about?" Then he nodded like she'd given him a clue. "Oh. *That's* why she left so abruptly. Wait. What happened in the bathroom?"

Ashleigh replayed her interaction with Jordyn, but to her annoyance, Chase laughed heartily.

She scowled. "It wasn't funny."

His laughter died down. "I'm sorry. I was just picturing Jordyn getting angry—which, believe me, I've seen plenty of times. But jumping to my defense? That's priceless." He glanced Ashleigh's way, his lips quirking up. "You have to admit, it was sweet of her to want to protect me from you."

"Protect *you* from *me?*" That annoyed her even more than his laughter did. *He* was the one who'd come up with the entire scheme.

He nodded, evidently missing her mood completely. "Yeah. You can be pretty dangerous, in case you didn't know."

Her eyebrows rose. "Really. How so?"

As he looked her way, his expression changed to one of

caution. Guess he'd finally caught on that she didn't find this funny, although she actually kind of did. She just wasn't going to make it easy for him.

"Uh," he stammered, "you know, the way you're so beautiful and intelligent and selfless, yet you've drawn a bright red line between us, keeping me away."

That made no sense, but she didn't care because she was stuck on his description of her as beautiful, intelligent, and selfless. Was that really what he thought about her or was he trying to butter her up to get her to go along with his plan? "Uh-huh."

"What? You disagree?"

Laughter bubbled up her throat. She couldn't help it. This was all so ridiculous.

Chase pulled off of the road and parked his Lamborghini, which was when Ashleigh noticed that from their vantage point they could see many houses adorned with Christmas lights. Some twinkled while others stayed a steady red, green, blue, and yellow. Others had white or clear lights and many trees were wrapped in lights as well.

Chase had left the car running, which pumped heat into the small space. Nice and cozy, and with the festive atmosphere, Ashleigh relaxed.

Chase reached behind Ashleigh's seat to the small shelf-like area behind her and retrieved a dark brown wicker basket with a lid, setting the basket on his lap.

"What's that?"

Lifting the basket's lid, he grinned. "Thought you might like some refreshments on our drive."

Curious, she watched as he took out a thermos and two mugs and then a small box. He opened the box, revealing four beautifully decorated Christmas cookies. He handed her a napkin and offered her a cookie. "Got them from Sprinkles of Joy. Gage boxed them up himself."

Ashleigh smiled. Leave it to Chase to use a sweet treat to break through her frustration. He was familiar with her sweet tooth—something she'd been trying to overcome but hadn't had a lot of success with. She thought about the treats he used to bring her, just because. Sometimes cookies, sometimes flowers, sometimes a book that he knew she'd been wanting to read. He'd been so thoughtful.

Thrusting those memories aside, she lifted a Santa Claus cookie out of the box and set it on her napkin. Chase chose a snowman cookie.

"Care for some hot chocolate?" he asked with a twinkle in his eyes as he set the box aside and opened the thermos.

"I'd love some. Thank you."

The thought of standing in front of him while a man pronounced them husband and wife sent a shiver of delight cascading over her. Marrying him was something she'd pictured many times when they'd been dating, which had made it all the more devastating when he'd left. Only problem was, it would all be for pretend. She wasn't sure her heart could take that.

She took the mug of hot chocolate he offered, then blew across the steaming liquid before taking a careful sip. It was hot, but not burning hot. "Mmm. Mint chocolate. My favorite."

He smiled. "I know it's your favorite."

Of course he did. "Did you get it from Gage too?"

He laughed. "No. The hot chocolate, I made myself."

Smirking, she said, "You never used to cook back in the day. Maybe pretend-marrying you wouldn't be such a bad thing after all."

His eyebrows shot up. "Are you saying you'll do it?"

"No."

Now he frowned. "So, you're saying you won't?"

She laughed. "I'm saying you need to convince me." Is that what she wanted? For him to talk her into it? Why would she ever agree? It was too much to ask.

CHAPTER 26

*H*ow could he convince her? Chase had no idea. He wasn't even sure he *wanted* to convince her. Maybe she was right and they should just forget the whole thing. His mom would just have to be happy with the thought that he was engaged without ever seeing it come to fruition, though that saddened him enormously. His wealth couldn't cure her, and the only thing that would bring her happiness was just out of reach. Unless he could persuade Ashleigh to put aside her trepidation and jump into it.

"You hurt me," she said out of the blue. At least it was out of the blue to him. Clearly, it had been on *her* mind.

It didn't take a genius to know what she was talking about, and hearing her state the words he'd known were lingering in her heart made him feel terrible.

He set his mug on the dashboard and twisted to face her,

which wasn't easy in the close confines of his Lamborghini. "I'm sorry, Ashleigh. When I left, I was only thinking about myself."

She nodded like she already knew this. "Did you ever miss me? Or even think about me?"

The intensity in her eyes told him how much she wanted to hear that he did. But the truth was, he'd been so focused on starting his business, he'd thought of nothing else. Now though, he hadn't been able to get her out of his mind.

"At first, yeah, I did think about you, but then I got so caught up in my new business that I slept, ate, and breathed it."

She nodded like she got it, but he could tell it didn't assuage her wounds.

Needing her to know he meant it, he said, "If I could go back, I would do it differently." Would he though? Because he was thrilled with the business he'd built.

"How?" she asked. "How would you do it differently?"

That was a tough one. He smiled softly. "I don't know, but I would definitely be more sensitive to you."

"Like not tell me I mean nothing?" Her voice shook on the last word.

"Nothing? What are you talking about? I never said you mean nothing."

Her mouth fell open as she made a scoffing sound. "You said, and I quote, 'There's nothing for me in Emerald Falls.'" She stared at him hard, unshed tears shimmering in her eyes. "Obviously you meant me."

He tried to recall that day but he couldn't remember exactly what he'd said. All he remembered was being excited to start his career after earning his degree.

Could he have said that to her? It was possible. But he hadn't meant it the way she'd taken it. And the idea that she'd believed that for all these years... It tore at him.

"That's not what I meant," he said lamely. What an idiot he'd been.

She looked away from him.

He was going about this all wrong. He was supposed to be convincing her to pretend-marry him on Christmas, not dwelling on the past.

It felt good to finally talk about the root of her deep hurt, although it seemed as if Chase didn't quite get it. At least she'd gotten it out there.

The moon cast enough light for Ashleigh to see Chase's face. His forehead was creased and his expression was pained.

"Ash," he said, drawing her eyes back to his face. "That's not what I meant, okay? Of course you're not nothing. You're a very special person." He shook his head. "I'm sorry that you...that you thought that's what I meant. I...I would never say that."

Though it was nice to hear his apology, the memory of that conversation still brought a sharp jab to her heart.

Although as she looked at his perplexed expression, she had to ask herself if she'd misunderstood what he'd meant back then. Although even if she had, it didn't lessen the pain of him walking away from her without a backward glance. The only consolation was that he hadn't left her for another girl.

Lost in their own thoughts, they were both silent as they sipped at their mugs.

"Can we talk about the wedding?" he asked.

The shift in topic jarred Ashleigh, but she knew they had to face what was happening right then. "What about it?"

He chuckled. "What's keeping you from agreeing to a Christmas wedding?" He said it as if they were planning on getting married and she just wanted to wait a little longer.

The absurdity of it made a laugh climb her throat. She didn't even try to suppress it. "Uh, where to start? How about the fact that we never agreed to a fake wedding? Or how about the fact that we'd be taking our lies to our families to the next level?" She tapped her chin. "Do I need to come up with more or is that reason enough?"

"No, I get it. I do. And I'm not super comfortable with putting on a wedding that's just a show. But my mom, she's not doing well, Ash."

The genuine emotion in his voice and on his face touched Ashleigh. She'd seen for herself that Sheila hadn't looked well, and she'd noticed that the only time she'd truly perked up was when she'd talked about the wedding.

"I'm sorry about your mom, Chase, I really am. It breaks my heart to see you going through this." Which reminded her of her confrontation with Jordyn, which made her think of an important point. "I'm not saying I'll do the wedding, but if we do it, can we at least tell Melanie and Jordyn the truth?"

His eyebrows tugged together as he looked downward. After a moment he lifted his gaze to hers. "If that's what it will take to get you to agree, then yes. We can tell those two. But no one else."

Okay. Maybe that changed things. Still, it would be a huge deal to have a pretend wedding. They would keep it small, but those closest to her would be there. Some would be happy for her and some would think she was nuts, but all of them would be deceived. She would have to get used to that idea.

Wait. Was she actually considering it?

Yes. Yes, she was.

"What are you thinking?" Chase asked.

Not quite ready to admit her thoughts, she bit off the head of her Santa cookie and slowly chewed. After she swallowed, she stared into those green eyes that had captured her heart years ago and said, "I'll do it."

CHAPTER 27

*C*hase couldn't believe she'd agreed to marry him in two weeks. Well, pretend-marry him. Still, it was incredible that she'd said yes. It was almost as exciting as an actual acceptance to a proposal would be. Except that it was nothing like that.

"Really?" he asked, just to make sure she wasn't playing with him.

She nodded, her face serious. "Yeah. I mean, it's for a good cause, right? And it's not real. I'll just…" she flung one hand outward, "pretend we're in a play or something."

Acting. Yeah, that's all it would be. Except that Chase found himself more and more drawn to her. Like, *really* drawn to her. Like, wanting-to-rekindle-their-relationship drawn to her. "Right."

Narrowing her eyes, she asked, "What's wrong?"

She knew him so well. Too well, apparently. "Nothing. Just surprised you agreed."

She stared at him like she knew he wasn't telling the truth. Which he wasn't, but he couldn't tell her what he was really thinking. Not after she'd made him promise to keep it platonic. A platonic wedding. That would be interesting.

"Can we kiss at the wedding?" The words came out of his mouth before he could think it through.

She scrunched up her face like he'd asked her to kiss a frog. "I guess we'll have to if we want to make it look legit."

He hadn't realized kissing him would be such a burden, but the fact that she thought it was only emphasized his decision to keep his feelings to himself. Why muddy the waters with emotions? This was complicated enough.

"Now that we have that out of the way," he said, ready to move on to practical matters, "what do we need to do to get ready?"

Her eyes widened like she'd just realized the wedding was really going to happen. Like panic was beginning to replace her calm agreement. "Hold on a sec. I, uh, I need to talk to Melanie first."

He could give her that. It was the least he could do. In the meantime, they could hang out, right?

"Can you take me home?" she asked, putting an end to the hope that she actually liked to spend time with him.

"Sure." He opened his door and poured out the rest of his hot chocolate, then put everything back in the basket, stowed the basket behind the seat, then put his car in gear and headed toward Ashleigh's house. "Can we get together tomorrow and hash out the details? I mean," he chuckled nervously, "there are a lot of things to get done over the next two weeks."

He purposely didn't look at her when he said this. No reason to let her drag him into her panic-vortex.

"Yeah. Sure."

Okay. She was still on board. Good.

They drove the rest of the way in silence, and when they reached her house, she fairly leapt from his car before he had a chance to turn off the engine.

"See you tomorrow!" he called to her retreating back.

She did a hand wave without turning to look at him.

Ashleigh was in a panic, but she knew Melanie would talk her off of the ledge. Either that or she'd convince her to jump while she still could. After all, very few people knew about the engagement and only Sheila knew about the wedding. It wasn't too late to back out. Except that it would crush Sheila.

"You're home," Melanie said when Ashleigh stepped inside and closed the door behind her.

"Yeah."

"Where'd you go? I mean, you kind of disappeared."

Oh yeah. She'd forgotten that she'd snuck out, worried that if Melanie saw Chase she would verbally attack him. What would Melanie do once she heard the truth?

She glanced behind her, toward the closed door where she heard Chase's cute car speeding away on the other side of it. "Chase and I went on a drive."

Melanie rolled her eyes, making it clear what she thought of *that*. "And?"

"And what?"

"And, what now? I can see something's up. Your eyes are all wide and panicked-looking." She sighed as pity filled her face. "Did he break the engagement already?"

"Rude."

Melanie's lips curled into a look of disdain. "It could happen, Ash. That's what worries me. I mean, he left once before."

Okay. Time to tell her the truth—and boy was she glad Chase had agreed they could tell Melanie and Jordyn. Otherwise it would have been a hellacious two weeks.

She took Melanie's hand and led her to the couch. "I have to tell you something."

Looking intrigued, Melanie followed Ashleigh to the couch and sat beside her. "What?"

"Before I tell you, you have to agree to two things."

"What?" Her tone was filled with suspicion.

"First, you have to keep this a secret, and second, you can't judge."

"Oh no. What happened? I know you can't be pregnant because it's been less than a week that you and Chase have been going out, and before that you haven't been out with anyone in weeks."

162

Her man-fast. Oh yeah. Guess that was over.

"Do you promise?"

Melanie flung her hands upwards. "Of course. Now, tell me what's going on."

So she did. Starting from the beginning and telling her everything that had happened, ending with her agreement to have the wedding in two weeks.

Melanie's mouth hung open in disbelief. "You're crazy. Do you know that? Totally bonkers."

"Yes. I'm well aware."

"Okay. Just so we're clear."

Ashleigh laughed. She couldn't help it. The whole thing was insane, but at least Melanie hadn't called anyone in a white coat to come haul her away. "So," Ashleigh asked, "Now what?"

"Now we need to plan a wedding."

CHAPTER 28

*N*ow that he'd agreed to tell the truth to his sister, Chase was eager to talk to her. But he had to do it where there was no chance their mom would overhear. He parked his Lamborghini and went into the house. Right into a Jordyn-storm.

"There you are," she said, her voice filled with fury.

He took a step back. "What's wrong?"

She glanced toward their mom, who was curled up on the couch with a blanket, her face serene. "Mom just told me that you and Ashleigh are getting married on *Christmas*." She glared at him. "Why? What's the hurry?"

This would be the perfect time to tell her the truth, but he had to get her by herself.

"Leave him alone, Jordyn," their mom said. "This has nothing to do with you."

Jordyn spun around, but must have thought better of saying what was on her mind, because she turned back to Chase and huffed a loud scoffing sound before stomping out of the room and down the hall to her bedroom.

"Sit down," his mom said, patting the cushion beside her.

He did as she asked.

"How are you doing?" she asked.

Now that Ashleigh was on board, he was doing much better, although he couldn't completely tamp down the guilt he felt at lying to his mom. At least Jordyn would know the truth. "I'm great."

"What about Ashleigh? How is she feeling about a Christmas wedding?"

He couldn't tell his mom exactly how Ashleigh felt because he wasn't completely sure himself, but she'd agreed to it, which was all that mattered. "She's good with it."

His mom's face lit up. "I'm so relieved to hear that." Her smile grew. "And I'm *so* excited."

They chatted about how the day might go, and after his mom headed off to bed, Chase knocked on Jordyn's door.

"Who is it?" she asked as if there could be a long list of visitors.

"It's Chase," he said, his voice soft.

A moment later she opened the door, then turned and walked to her bed, sitting on the edge.

He walked in, closed the door behind him, and sat beside her. "We need to talk." He spoke just above a whisper.

"Did Mom go to bed?"

He nodded. "Yeah. And I don't want her to hear this."

Her eyebrows furrowed and then released. "What's up?"

"Can you keep a secret?"

She gave him a pained expression. "What do you think?"

"Is that a yes?"

She nodded. "Yes."

"Okay." He glanced toward the door as if their mom might be on the other side with a glass pressed up against the wood. His voice dropped to a whisper. "The wedding isn't real."

"What?!"

"Shhh." He pressed a finger to his lips and glared at her. "Keep it down."

"What?" she asked again in a mock-whisper.

He explained his plan, watching her expression go from complete disbelief to dawning understanding to grudging acceptance. "You know you're both nutjobs, right?"

Chase pursed his lips. "I'm doing it for Mom."

"I know." She frowned. "Now I feel like a jerk for what I said to your *fiancée*." She did air quotes over the word.

He smiled as he shook his head. "It's fine. She understands. And it was her idea to tell you and Melanie the truth."

She tilted her head. "Points for Ashleigh."

He laughed. "Right?"

"Are you sure about this? I mean, I know Mom is beyond thrilled, but it's kind of a major event to pull off when it's fake." She grimaced. "Plus, how do you think everyone will feel when they find out they were tricked?"

Hearing that magnified the guilt Chase had been trying to quash. He didn't relish the idea of lying to friends and family, but that wasn't going to stop him from making his mom's one dying wish come true. "Once Mom's...well, once she's gone, people will forgive us."

At the mention of their mother's terminal state, Jordyn nodded. "Right." She inhaled sharply. "So, what can I do to help?"

He loved his sister. First she stood up to a possible inter-loper—Ashleigh—and now she was stepping up to help in any way she could.

"I don't know," he said, then he chuckled. "I've never planned a wedding before."

"I know a wedding planner that can take the reins."

He nodded. "That would be awesome." He would much rather hire someone to figure this out. Besides, it would be a much nicer wedding if he stepped out of the way. He would let Ashleigh know so she could get involved as much or as little as she liked.

Okay, why was he starting to get excited like he was really marrying her? At least she'd given permission to kiss her at the ceremony.

"Why are you smiling like an idiot, all of a sudden?" Jordyn asked.

He laughed. "Inside joke."

Jordyn smiled and shook her head. "Fine."

Glad he'd been able to get back in his sister's good graces, he told her goodnight and headed to bed, eager to see Ashleigh the next day.

CHAPTER 29

"Wait," Taylor said the next morning at the library after Ashleigh told her the big news, "you're getting *married?* On *Christmas?* That's in *two weeks!* Wait, *married?!*"

And so it began. She still had to break the news to so many people, but at least she had Melanie's support. "I know it sounds crazy—"

Taylor cut her off. "*Sounds* crazy. It *is* crazy." She shook her head. "Whatever, Ash. You do you."

She hated for everyone to think she was nuts. She had to explain. "His mom is dying. That's why we're doing it so soon."

Taylor scrunched up her nose like this was too sad to think about. "Oh."

"Anyway, I want you to come, so I wanted to give you a head's up."

That brightened her mood. "Yeah. Of course I'll come. And I'll bring Seth." She grinned. "Maybe your wedding will give him ideas."

"You want to marry him?" She hadn't meant to sound so surprised, but with all the complaining she'd heard from Taylor, it did surprise her.

"Not right now, but, you know, maybe eventually."

"You don't sound sure."

"I'm not, but he could at least ask."

Ashleigh laughed and shook her head. "I'd better get back to work."

It was a busy day at the library, which was good because Ashleigh didn't want to think about her upcoming pretend nuptials, but when Chase got to her house that evening, she had no choice but to face reality.

"Come on in," she said, no longer nervous for him to run in to Melanie. In fact, Ashleigh had made dinner with the idea that Melanie could join them, but Gage was taking her and Avery out.

"You look nice," he said with an appraising look.

As much as Ashleigh appreciated the compliment, she didn't want him trying to woo her. That was all she needed— for him to muddy this up by acting like he really cared about her. "You know, I'm not going to back out of the wedding so you don't have to do stuff like that."

He seemed taken aback. "Stuff like what?"

"Say nice things." Why was she defensive all of a sudden?

Frowning, he said, "Okay. I'll keep my thoughts to myself."

"Good."

"Hi, Chase," Melanie said as she walked into the living room. Her tone was friendly but not overly so.

He turned to her. "Hey."

"I hear congratulations are in order." Then she smirked. *Way to go, sis.*

Chase took it like a champ, chuckling before saying, "Thanks. All my dreams will be coming true."

They both laughed, but Ashleigh didn't. Then again, Chase was probably trying to downplay everything. Which he should, because it didn't mean anything. To either of them. Right? It was all about making Sheila happy. Ashleigh had to get her head in the game.

Melanie was looking at Ashleigh so she shoved a smile onto her lips and played along. "Yeah. It'll be my dream wedding."

"Oh," Chase said, turning to her, "that reminds me. Jordyn gave me the name of a wedding planner who can take care of the whole thing. So, I reached out to her. It's up to you to do as much or as little as you want."

"Okay." It was thoughtful of him to take care of it. Although he should, since the whole scheme was his idea.

"How many people are you thinking of inviting?" Melanie asked both of them.

"We should keep it small," Ashleigh said. "You know, the fewer people to witness the charade the better."

"Good point," Chase said. "Small and intimate. Just family and close friends."

A knock sounded on the door.

"That must be Gage," Melanie said with a bright smile, again making Ashleigh long for her own true love.

Melanie went to the door and let Gage inside.

"Is that your Lamborghini?" Gage asked Chase after kissing Melanie hello.

Chase grinned. "Like it?"

"Uh, yeah."

"Gage drives a Camaro," Melanie added.

"Love those too," Chase said.

The men started talking about cars, and Melanie said to Ashleigh, "Help me get Avery ready."

Ashleigh knew Avery was already ready and playing in her room, so she knew Melanie wanted to talk to her. "Sure."

The two of them went down the hall, stopping outside Avery's open door. "Do you want me to tell Gage your news, or do you want to tell him?"

"You can tell him."

Melanie stared at her. "Are you sure about this? I mean, it's not too late to back out. You know, before you start telling everyone."

She'd already told Taylor and she didn't know how many people Sheila had told. Besides, she was committed to following through. "I'm sure." She laughed. "As sure as anyone can be in this situation."

"Okay." She collected Avery and the three of them went back to the living room where the men were still talking.

"Did Chase tell you his big news?" Melanie asked Gage when there was a pause in the conversation.

Gage looked at Chase. "News?"

Melanie smiled. "He and Ashleigh are getting married. On Christmas."

Gage's eyebrows shot up. "*This* Christmas?"

Chase nodded. "Yep."

"Not to be nosy, but how long have you guys known each other?"

Deciding she needed to practice her loving fiancée act, Ashleigh stood beside Chase and slipped an arm around his waist. "We dated years ago and now we've reconnected."

His arm went around her shoulders and he gazed at her lovingly, clearly ready to practice their routine as well. "When we saw each other again, we knew we'd made a mistake in breaking up."

Holding back a scoffing sound—she'd never wanted to break up in the first place—Ashleigh worked to reflect Chase's smile. "When it's right it's right."

Gage nodded and clapped Chase on the back. "Congratulations." He paused a beat. "Who's doing your wedding cake?"

Ashleigh suppressed a laugh. Gage owned Sprinkles of Joy bakery and never passed up an opportunity to bake something for someone.

"No one yet," she said.

He smiled warmly. "I'll make it. It'll be my wedding present to the two of you."

Melanie slipped her hand into his and rested her head on his shoulder. "That's so sweet, Gage."

"Yes," Ashleigh said, "thank you."

Chase smiled. "Thanks, man. That would be amazing."

When Gage, Melanie, and Avery had left, Ashleigh invited Chase into the eat-in kitchen. "Dinner's just about ready."

"Smells delicious." Then he slammed his mouth shut. "Sorry. I didn't mean to compliment you."

Feeling like a jerk for her earlier comment, Ashleigh looked at the floor, letting her long hair fall in front of her face. Time to apologize. Pushing her hair out of her face, she lifted her head and met Chase's green-eyed gaze. "Forget what I said, okay?"

He laughed. "Which part?"

"Where I said not to say nice things. I mean, you don't have to, but if you do I won't bite your head off."

Nodding solemnly, he said, "Good to know."

Trying not to roll her eyes, Ashleigh turned her back on Chase and took out plates, glasses, and silverware, setting them on the counter.

"I can set the table," he offered.

She turned around and smiled at him. "Thank you." While he did that, she put together the salad and carried it over to the table. Moments later the timer chimed.

"Please sit," she said as she took the chicken casserole out of the oven and set it on a hot pad on the table.

They served themselves, and as they ate, Ashleigh asked for the name of the wedding planner.

"Do you want to help plan it?" Chase asked before taking a large bite of casserole.

Did she? She had enjoyed planning the fundraiser—was that only the week before? It seemed ages ago. But planning a wedding was way out of her comfort zone. Besides, if she was deeply involved, would it make it feel too real, like she was actually getting married? Would it mess with her head?

"I'll meet with her," she said, deciding she wanted to have *some* input. "Just to see what she's thinking of." A new thought occurred to her. "Did you give her a budget?" How much was he willing to spend on this pretend wedding anyway?

"Kind of."

"What does that mean?"

"I told her I want to keep it under thirty grand."

Ashleigh nearly choked. "Thirty thousand dollars?"

"*Under* thirty grand."

"I should hope so. I mean, this is a *pretend* wedding."

"I know."

If he was willing to spend that kind of money, maybe the Bookmobile should go back on the table.

He rolled his eyes. "Anyway, she'll let me know if there's a need for more." He paused. "Which reminds me, you need a dress."

She'd been too overwhelmed with the idea of the wedding to consider the details. "Right."

"Do you know where to get one?"

"I'm sure I can figure it out. The problem is, if they need to alter it, that takes time."

He frowned. "Oh."

"Is that going to be a problem?" This was hard enough without any roadblocks.

"You tell me. I mean, can you make it work?"

What if she said no? What would happen then? Would they have to postpone? But she'd committed to this. "Of course. I'll make it happen." Chase's outrageous budget would smooth the way.

"Great!"

As she looked at him, it suddenly occurred to her that two weeks from that day, she would be standing in front of him exchanging vows. With the man who had broken her heart.

Suddenly she couldn't meet his gaze.

CHAPTER 30

*I*t was weird, planning this wedding with Ashleigh. They were doing the exact same things they would do if it were real, except for the most important part—the part where they were deliriously in love.

He watched her as she arranged her napkin on her lap, seeming to avoid looking at him.

"Ashleigh?"

Her gaze flicked to his, revealing her vulnerability, like she was trusting him to do this right, trusting him to make sure she got out of this with her heart intact.

At that moment, seeing how truly vulnerable she was, he vowed to keep his feelings to himself. It wouldn't be right for him to say or do anything that would lead her to believe there could be a future for them, not when he had no idea if that was possible. He refused to risk hurting her again. She deserved so much better than that.

"What?" she asked.

What had he been about to say? Whatever it was, he had to keep things light, keep things platonic. He smiled. "Can I get this recipe? It's delicious."

She stared at him like she didn't believe the soft tone he used when he said her name matched the words he was saying now. Then she smiled. "Of course."

Ready to stay on safe topics, he asked, "How are things at the library?"

She seemed to relax. "Great! Today I ordered two computers and about a dozen new books."

They chatted about both of their careers as they ate, and when they were done, Ashleigh brought out a plate of lemon cookies.

Chase took a bite of one, the taste bringing back memories of Ashleigh baking them for him. "Do you still take plates of treats to your neighbors at Christmas?" He'd helped deliver them one year.

Now that they were keeping things on a non-romantic level, Ashleigh was enjoying herself much more. Although she couldn't completely suppress her deep attraction to Chase.

"Yep, and I've added mint chocolate chip cookies to my repertoire."

He laughed. "You still do fudge and sugar cookies, don't you?"

She nodded. "Of course. Those are favorites."

Grinning, he asked, "Do you give some to Gage?"

That brought on a laugh. "I wouldn't dare. Not with the amazing cookies he makes at Sprinkles of Joy."

"It was nice of him to offer to bake our wedding cake."

Our wedding cake. Like this was real. She wished he would stop saying things like that. "It's not a real wedding, you know."

An emotion Ashleigh couldn't name flashed across his face. "I know."

Time to wrap this up. She stood and started clearing the dishes.

Chase was by her side moments later. "Let me help you clean up."

Though she appreciated the sentiment, she needed him to go. It was too hard to spend all this time with him while convincing her heart that none of this was real. "I've got it." She smiled. "Anyway, I think it's time to say goodnight."

His eyebrows bunched. "Okay."

He looked kind of hurt, which made Ashleigh feel guilty, but she shoved the feeling down, and when he turned and walked toward the front door, she followed.

He stopped at the door, his hand on the knob. "I won't be available tomorrow, but can we get together on Friday?"

Did they need to? Not that she hated the idea of spending time with him, but darn it! It was hard to be with him and know there was nothing there. No feelings. No commitment. At least on his part. She definitely had feelings—feelings that refused to be subdued.

He frowned. "If we're telling people we're getting married, we should probably be seen together."

Much as she hated to admit it, he was right. "Okay. Friday it is."

He flashed a smile, but she could tell it was forced. Was he hating this as much as she was?

Chase hated that Ashleigh could barely tolerate his presence. And it seemed to be getting worse the more time they spent together. Honestly, if he felt the same way, it would make it easier. But he was having the opposite reaction—the more time he spent with her, the more time he *wanted* to spend with her. That was unexpected. He hadn't gone into this thinking that would happen, but there it was.

"All right," he said, not wanting to torture her any longer than necessary, "I'll pick you up for dinner Friday at six thirty."

She nodded, but her smile was strained. "See you then."

He opened the door and walked out. He'd barely stepped off the porch before he heard the deadbolt turn in Ashleigh's front door.

What she didn't know was that he was free the next night. In telling her he was busy, he'd kind of been testing her to see her reaction. Would she be disappointed or relieved? He was the one who'd been disappointed when not only had she been relieved they wouldn't be getting together the next night, but that she had been reluctant to go out the night after that.

Sighing, he got into his Lamborghini and backed out of her driveway. Then he softly chuckled. Most women were eager to go out with him. Not Ashleigh. One of many things that drew her to him. He mentally listed other qualities of hers that he liked: selflessness, intelligence, empathetic, hard-working, not to mention gorgeous.

Too bad he'd blown it with her six years earlier. He was paying for it now.

CHAPTER 31

"I'm envisioning a Winter Wonderland," Deena, the wedding planner, said the next day when Ashleigh met with her at Deena's office after work. She'd gotten off early for the meeting, and it wasn't until she'd been standing in front of Deena that she'd realized how odd it might appear that Chase wasn't there with her. Fortunately, she'd managed to come up with an excuse as to why her husband-to-be wasn't involved in planning.

"No worries," Deena had said with a smile. "It's not uncommon for the groom to leave all the planning up to the bride."

At that word—*bride*—Ashleigh felt a jolt go through her. *She* was the bride. And this was her wedding. A fake wedding, but the wedding planner didn't know that and she was into full-bore planning mode.

"Do you like that idea?" Deena asked. "The Winter Wonderland theme? Or do you have something else in mind? I mean, it will be on Christmas so we can go with a Christmas theme, but that seems so trite, so overdone." Her arms were flailing about as she said this. Ashleigh had to take a step back to keep from being clocked in the head.

"Winter Wonderland sounds good." In all reality, she was willing to let Deena do all of the planning. She just wanted to make sure the woman didn't do anything crazy, like have people dressed as snowmen serving hors d'oeuvres. Other than that, the less she was involved, the better. That would make it easier to keep a chasm between reality and the wedding charade.

They discussed how Deena would decorate the venue, which Chase had somehow managed to reserve. No doubt with a large infusion of cash. What venue was still available for Christmas in the middle of December, anyway? Whatever. That wasn't Ashleigh's concern. She just needed to be the blushing bride.

Deena had several food samples for Ashleigh to try. They sat at a table as Ashleigh sampled the options. She picked the Salmon and Filet Mignon, along with a number of sides.

"My friend Gage is providing the cake," she told Deena.

"Oh, but I have someone I prefer to use."

All of this was for show, but her friendship with Gage was real. "No. Gage owns a bakery and he's doing the cake."

Deena's hands went up. "Okay. Fine." Ashleigh scooted her chair backwards.

They looked at pictures of bridal bouquets. Ashleigh's colors would be red and green. Those weren't her favorite colors, but she was fine with them and they worked for a Christmas wedding. The bouquet she chose was a mix of white and red roses with bits of baby's breath and holly berries.

"How many bridesmaids will there be?" Deena asked.

She hadn't considered that. Of course she would ask Melanie to be her maid of honor. For the rest of her bridal party, she would ask Jordyn and Taylor. It would be a small group, but she wanted to keep it small. Even as she pictured the women who would support her, guilt sliced through her.

To keep herself from bursting into spasms of shame, she pictured the absolute joy that would grace Sheila's face that day. She would be ecstatic to see Chase happily married.

I'm her Christmas Angel, she told herself over and over.

"I'll have a maid of honor and two bridesmaids," she told Deena.

"Very good. And the groom will have a best man and two groomsmen?"

If you say so. "Yeah." She'd let Chase know how many men he had to come up with.

"We will have the best photographer and of course a videographer," Deena said with a proud smile.

Ashleigh almost told her they didn't need any of those. Why document a lie? But of course it would be expected and not having them would raise all kinds of questions. "Great."

Deena handed her a flash drive. "Here are samples from

several bands. You and the groom choose your favorite and I will hire the band."

This woman thought of everything, much to Ashleigh's relief. "Okay."

"I will need to know your decision by Saturday."

Guess the activity for the next night's date was decided. "All right."

"That's it. Call me if you have any questions."

Ashleigh's head was spinning. She stood from the table, her legs a little wobbly, and stumbled out the door.

Once home, she had to cool her heels until Melanie got home two hours later before she could ask her to be her maid of honor.

"I guess so," she said, her tone reluctant, "I mean, I don't really like pretending, but of course I want to support you."

"I'm pretending as if this whole wedding is an elaborate play. You always wanted to act, didn't you?"

Melanie looked at her like she was batty. "No. I never wanted to act."

"But you can take it up, right?"

Melanie burst out laughing and walked away, shaking her head.

Ashleigh trailed after her. "Is that a yes?"

Melanie turned and faced her. "For you, yes."

Throwing her arms around her, Ashleigh whispered, "Thank you." Fortunately, Taylor would be eager to say yes. And Ashleigh assumed Jordyn would be on board. It was for her mother, after all.

That evening, she spoke to both women, getting Taylor's enthusiastic agreement. Jordyn's response, on the other hand, was much calmer and more measured. Luke-warm, even.

"You know this isn't real," Ashleigh felt the need to remind her.

"I do know," Jordyn said, "and I'm grateful you're doing this for my mom, but the whole thing just stinks. The cancer, the pretending, all of it."

"I know." The reminder that Sheila was terminal put everything back into perspective. Still, Ashleigh would be glad when she had Chase by her side to face it all. She was exhausted by all the preparations she'd had to deal with that day. Not to mention the guilt that always lingered around the edges of her mind.

She was ready to get the whole thing over with. Except for one thing.

Once the wedding was over and Sheila, well, once the charade was no longer necessary, would Ashleigh ever see Chase again? They'd spent every day together for nearly a week, and to her dismay, she discovered that she really, *really* missed seeing him.

CHAPTER 32

uch to Chase's surprise, as he drove to Ashleigh's house on Friday evening, he found himself impatient to see her. He pictured her face and thought about her smile. It hadn't been that long since he'd seen her—forty-eight hours to be precise—so why did he miss her so much?

Not wanting to read too much into it, he focused on driving, and when he got to her house, he lifted the vase of flowers from the floor of his Lamborghini and carried it to the front door.

After a brisk knock, he heard footsteps approaching. A moment later Ashleigh opened the door, a smile on her face. Chase's heart did a little leap of happiness. She didn't look like she was put out by having to see him. Maybe there was hope after all. Either that or she was sucking it up.

He held out the vase of flowers. "I brought these for you."

"Thank you. They're beautiful." She took them from him and stepped back, allowing him to enter.

It was quiet inside. "Is Melanie here?"

She set the vase on the coffee table, then turned and faced him. "No. She's out with Gage."

He nodded. Good. A moment alone. "How did your meeting with Deena go?"

Ashleigh laughed and shook her head. "It was fine, but there are *so* many details. How is everything going to get done in time?"

He grinned. "That's why I hired her. She'll make it happen."

"That reminds me…" She went to her purse, which was on the couch, and dug through it. A moment later she held a flash drive in her hand. "We have homework."

"What?"

Holding the up drive, she said, "Deena gave this to me. It has music from several bands. We need to choose one and tell her by tomorrow."

Thinking about the next day brought a smile to Chase's face—because he had a surprise for Ashleigh. One that he hoped she would appreciate.

She must have read the look on his face, because she asked, "What?"

He had to work on his poker face. "Just ready to listen to some tunes."

"Okay."

He could tell she didn't believe him. That was fine. "First though, we need provisions."

"What did you have in mind?"

"Does Eats & Treats deliver?"

"Yeah, I think they do."

He pulled his phone out of his pocket. "What sounds good to you?" After a brief discussion, he called the diner and placed their order, then he tucked his phone away. "Okay. Let's get started."

"Oh," she said with a grimace, "by the way. I'm going to have a maid of honor and two bridesmaids, so you'll need a best man and two groomsmen."

Chase immediately knew who he'd ask—his good friends Josh Reynolds, Brian Foster, and Aaron Pearce. "No problem."

"Good." Ashleigh sat on the couch and picked up the laptop that was sitting on the coffee table. He sat beside her as she booted up the laptop and inserted the flash drive. A moment later, music filled the room.

"This band sounds good," Chase said, looking at Ashleigh like they were trying to make an incredibly important decision. "What do you think?"

This felt surreal to Ashleigh. And so, so wrong. How could they act like this was normal? It wasn't. Not in the least. Forcing her head into the game, she feigned a smile. "They sound good."

A moment later another song started.

"This sounds like another band," Chase said. "I don't like it as much as the last one."

Kind of impressed that he was taking this so seriously while at the same time acutely annoyed that he was taking this so seriously, Ashleigh frowned.

"What?" he asked. "Do you like them?"

It doesn't matter, she wanted to shout, but once again, she smiled politely. "They're okay, but I like the other one too." In reality, they sounded very similar.

"Okay. Let's see what the next one sounds like."

A new song came on, but this was a song Ashleigh knew well. It was *Somebody That I Used to Know* by Gotye. When Chase had left her she'd listened to it over and over.

Desperately trying to smash the melancholy that surged through her, when she heard the line "Make out like it never happened and that we were nothing," she couldn't stop the intense feelings that had plagued her for months after Chase had left from overwhelming her.

Chase frowned at her, his forehead furrowing with grave concern. "What's wrong?"

To her horror, Ashleigh realized she was crying. Big, fat tears were rolling down her cheeks.

"Ashleigh. Tell me. Please."

She'd already told him that his words had made her feel like she meant nothing to him. There was no reason to bring it up again. Instead, a flash of realization settled over her. After going through this masquerade, Chase would leave her once more and she would experience the same devastation again. Only it would be worse, because she would go through a wedding with him first. Fake, yes, but all too real.

"I can't do this," she blurted.

He smiled. "It's fine. We can listen to the bands later."

He wasn't getting her message. She needed him to understand, needed him to know that this wasn't going to work. She shook her head. "No. That's not what I meant."

Understanding seemed to dawn on him as his eyes went wide and his lips parted. "Wait. Are you saying what I think—"

She cut him off. "Yes. That's *exactly* what I'm saying. The engagement is off." She pulled the gorgeous ring off of her finger and set it on the coffee table before standing. "Please see yourself out." She hurried out of the living room before heading down the hall, desperately hoping he would do as she asked and leave.

Guilt zinged through her at the disappointment Sheila would experience when she heard the news, but Ashleigh had to protect her own heart. If she didn't, who would?

She still loved Chase. Trying to convince herself otherwise was futile.

She went into her bedroom and closed and locked the door before bursting into sobs that stole her breath away.

CHAPTER 33

Chase was stunned. More than that, he was baffled. What had set Ashleigh off? Why had she changed her mind? And did she really mean it?

The doorbell rang. Momentarily confused as to who it could be, Chase answered the door. A woman in her twenties stood there.

Chase stared at her. "Can I help you?"

She held out a bag. "Your order."

He'd completely forgotten that they'd ordered a meal from Eats & Treats. "Oh. Right." He paid the bill, adding a generous tip, and took the bag.

She smiled. "Thanks." Then she turned and walked away.

Nodding absently, Chase closed the door. Holding the bag in his hand, he stood there dumbly. What was he supposed to do now?

Put the food on the counter, his mind commanded. Blinking several times, he mindlessly walked toward the kitchen, stopping beside the counter and setting the bag on the granite surface.

He was going to have to tell his mom that the wedding was off. Not just the wedding, but the engagement.

She would be crushed.

Maybe he could change Ashleigh's mind. He looked in the direction she'd gone, but he wasn't about to invade her sanctuary to demand an explanation.

Please see yourself out.

Ashleigh's words rang in his ears. She clearly had no desire to speak to him. He had to respect her wishes.

With great reluctance, he trudged to the front door, pausing before opening it, hoping against hope that she would come out and say she'd changed her mind. Hadn't she reassured him that she wouldn't back out?

He stood there for a full minute before quietly nodding his acceptance that she wouldn't be speaking to him. At least that night. With an audible sigh, he opened the door and stepped out into the cold December night.

Chase didn't go straight home. He couldn't. Not with the news written all over his face. His mom knew him too well. She would know something was amiss in paradise. So, he drove around until he was certain she would be asleep, then he snuck into the house like a wayward teenager, tiptoeing down the hall and into his bedroom. Breathing a sigh of relief that he hadn't run into his mom, when he heard a soft knock at his door, he closed his eyes and shook his head.

"Chase?"

It was Jordyn.

Grateful he had someone he could talk to about this, he let her into his room, closing the door behind her.

"How's it going?" she asked.

There was no easy way to say it. "Ashleigh's out."

Jordyn's eyes widened. "What? Why?"

Chase shook his head. "No idea."

Giving him a look that said *You know more than you think you do*, she asked, "Tell me what happened."

Still completely perplexed, he thought back to the evening. "We were listening to music by different bands for our wedding when she just started crying." The memory of seeing the tears streaming down Ashleigh's face sent a stab of sadness right to his heart. What had set her off? Was it something he had done?

"It was the song," Jordyn said as if she read his mind.

"The song?" he asked as he tugged on one ear. At least it wasn't *him*.

"Obviously, it reminded her of something sad."

Well, yeah. Now that he thought about it, it was kind of obvious. But what? What was so sad that it had made her want to back out of their fake engagement?

"What was the song?" Jordyn asked.

"I don't remember." And he'd left the flash drive at Ashleigh's house.

Jordyn threw up her hands and huffed a sigh. "You're useless, Chase. You know that?"

He was beginning to think the same thing. "Sorry." He watched as Jordyn paced the short distance from one side of his room to the other. "Can you stop pacing?"

She did, stopping in front of him and staring at him. "What's bothering you the most? That Mom's going to be disappointed or that Ashleigh dumped you?"

"Both." Of course he didn't want to disappoint his mom, but seeing Ashleigh in tears had gutted him.

Jordyn put her hands on her hips. "You need to talk to Ashleigh."

"I don't think she wants to see me."

Jordyn stared at him like he was an especially slow pupil. "Of course she does."

He tilted his head to the side and pursed his lips. "What makes you think that?" Why did women have to be so hard to figure out? Why couldn't they be like a computer program where you entered in a specific set of data and the information that came out was logical?

"Did she tell you she never wanted to see you again?"

The only thing she'd said was *Please let yourself out*. Not *I never want to see your ugly mug again* or *I wish you were dead* or anything else that implied she wished he'd take a long walk off a short pier. "No."

Jordyn lifted her hands up and smiled. "There you go."

"There I go?"

She shook her head like she believed he was hopeless, which he guessed he was. At least when it came to love.

She sat beside him on the bed. "You have to read between the lines, Chase."

"Okay. And what do those lines say? Or do I need special glasses to see them?"

She laughed. "Give her some time and then approach her to see what's going on."

"How much time? I mean, Christmas is in twelve days."

She shook her head. "Forget the wedding."

Was he supposed to read between the lines of Jordyn's comment now? He was so confused.

She must have been able to tell that he wasn't following, because she added, "For now. Forget about the wedding for now."

"Oh."

"Don't even mention it. Just focus on what's in her heart, what made her sad." Her eyebrows went up as she stared at him. "Can you do that, Chase?"

"Yeah. That I can do."

With a mission in mind, he told Jordyn goodnight and got ready for bed, all the while trying to figure out the best way to approach Ashleigh.

CHAPTER 34

*A*shleigh was the first one up the next morning. It wasn't difficult when she'd hardly slept. For hours after she'd gone to bed she'd replayed the day that Chase had told her he was leaving Emerald Falls, and by midnight she'd been emotionally wrung out and had finally fallen asleep only to wake again at five in the morning with an epiphany —the only way she would heal was to leave the past in the past and move forward.

How she would do *that* she had no idea.

She went into the kitchen and began a batch of pancakes. By the time the first batch was done, Melanie wandered into the kitchen, yawning.

"You're up early," Melanie said as she began setting the table.

"How was your date with Gage?"

Melanie took three plates out of the cabinet, stacked accompanying silverware on top of them, then carried it all to the table. "Wonderful. I love that man."

At least someone was happy. Ashleigh poured batter onto the griddle, then carried a plate of golden brown pancakes to the table. "Do you think the two of you will ever get married?" Now, why had she brought that up? She didn't want to think about weddings—her cancelled fake one or anyone else's.

"I hope so." Melanie sat down, her gaze falling to Ashleigh's naked left ring finger before she met Ashleigh's eyes. "Why aren't you wearing your ring?"

Ashleigh had worn it pretty much all the time since she'd gotten it. "I, uh, I forgot to put it on."

Melanie frowned. "Don't lie to me, Ash."

Oh, what was the use? If she couldn't tell her sister the truth, who could she tell? Sighing audibly, she went back to the griddle and flipped the pancakes, then turned and faced her sister. "I gave him the ring back."

Melanie's eyebrows shot up. "What?"

"Mommy!" Avery said, bounding into the room and jumping into Melanie's arms.

Glad for the distraction, Ashleigh turned her back on her sister and focused on the pancakes.

"We're not done talking," Melanie said before turning her attention to her daughter.

As far as Ashleigh was concerned, they *were* done talking. Mainly because she didn't know how she felt anymore. The light of a new day always gave her a fresh perspective. That, and the realization that she needed to let the past go.

A knock sounded at the door.

Who would come over this early? Had to be a salesperson, right? Either that or Chase.

Alarmed and excited all at the same time, Ashleigh called out "I'll get it," before Melanie had a chance to move from her chair.

"Wait!" Melanie commanded, stopping Ashleigh in her tracks while at the same time quieting Avery. They both looked at Melanie with wide eyes. Melanie narrowed hers. "Tell me what's going on."

Another knock.

Ignoring the door—he could wait—Ashleigh faced Melanie. "I told him I couldn't go through with it."

Melanie smiled. "Good for you."

Was it? Maybe it *was* good for her, but what about Sheila? Had Chase already broken *her* heart by telling her the engagement was off?

Now the doorbell rang.

Had to be Chase.

Ashleigh glanced toward the door. "I need to talk to him."

Melanie stood. "No, you don't. I'll tell him you're busy."

Was that what Ashleigh wanted? Honestly, she wasn't sure. But if she truly wanted to put the past behind her and truly forgive Chase for the hurt he'd caused, she would march to the door, open it wide, and face him.

Ashleigh set her jaw. "I'll talk to him."

Melanie heaved a sigh. "Fine."

Glad she didn't have to argue with her sister, who she knew only had her best interests at heart, Ashleigh strode to the door and reached for the knob. Then her heart started pounding. Chase stood on the other side of the door—it had to be him. Would he beg her to reconsider? Tell her she was right and they shouldn't pretend any longer? Or do something completely unexpected?

Bracing herself, she inhaled sharply before slowly releasing her breath, then she opened the door.

Yep. It was him. Handsome as sin, his green eyes directed at her, not wavering even a little.

"Good morning." His voice was low and sexy. Ashleigh knew he wasn't even trying to be so attractive, but she couldn't stop her heart from thundering with a longing that had gripped her all night long.

Seeing Ashleigh standing there, her blue eyes wide, her expression broadcasting her vulnerability, did something to Chase, and all of a sudden he wanted to drag her into his arms and promise that everything would be okay. But he couldn't do that, couldn't make a promise that he wasn't sure he could keep. It wouldn't be fair to Ashleigh or to himself. Instead, he tried to recall what he'd planned on saying, but every last word had fled his brain.

"What...," Ashleigh began, "what are you doing here?"

I'm here to convince you to reconsider, was what he wanted to say, but when he remembered Jordyn's advice to forget the engagement and just focus on Ashleigh and why she'd burst into tears, his mind clarified. "I wanted to make sure you're all right. I mean, you were really upset last night. I've...I've been worried about you."

Her expression softened and he knew he'd said the right thing.

She opened the door and swept her arm toward the interior. "Do you want to join us for breakfast? I'm making pancakes."

He glanced toward the kitchen. He couldn't see the 'us' she was referring to, but he could hear Avery's voice. Obviously it was Melanie and her daughter. He would have preferred to have Ashleigh all to himself, but at this point he would take whatever he could get.

He stepped inside. "Sure. Thank you."

She smiled, then turned and walked toward the kitchen. He followed, and when he saw Melanie wearing pajamas, he felt like an intruder and almost made an excuse to leave. Instead, he smiled brightly. "Good morning."

She scowled at him before arranging her face in a pleasant smile. "Hi."

All right. She wasn't a fan. That was okay. It was Ashleigh he had to please, not her sister. Although he wasn't an idiot. He knew Melanie's opinion of him could influence Ashleigh.

Wanting to show some sensitivity, he looked at Melanie and said, "Ashleigh invited me to join you, but I can go."

Melanie's eyebrows rose in clear surprise that he would ask her, then her gaze shot to Ashleigh, who stood behind Chase. He couldn't see Ashleigh's reaction, but when Melanie's eyes shifted to him, she smiled and said, "No, please join us."

Okay. So, Ashleigh really did want him to stay. Feeling optimistic, he smiled. "Thank you."

Ashleigh set a plate and utensils on the table for him, so he sat.

"I understand Ashleigh axed the engagement," Melanie said, staring hard at him.

CHAPTER 35

*A*shleigh wanted to kill her sister, which she tried to convey by throwing daggers with her eyes. Melanie completely ignored her. When Chase looked in Ashleigh's direction, she put the daggers away and smiled at him. "We're working it out." That elicited a look of surprise from Chase—he obviously had no idea any working out was going on since all that work was being done in Ashleigh's head.

"Oh really?" Melanie said, clearly wanting to prolong Ashleigh's suffering.

Chase's eyes went to Melanie, but he wisely said nothing.

Desperate to change the topic, Ashleigh asked, "Can we talk about something else?"

"Can I have more pancakes?" Avery asked, once again saving the day.

"Yes, you can." Ashleigh hadn't meant for her voice to

have manic enthusiasm, but that's what you got when relief built to a crescendo. She poured more batter onto the griddle. A sizzling sound filled the air. Keeping her back to the table, she watched as bubbles formed on the pancakes, then she flipped them over. Perfect. Chase would be impressed with her cooking.

Wait. Who cared if he was impressed? Eventually he would go back to Cupertino, back to his life as a successful entrepreneur, back to being a serial dater of beautiful women, back to forgetting all about her.

Catching herself in a deep frown, she perked up her lips, scooped the golden brown pancakes onto a plate, and carried it to the table, depositing one pancake onto Avery's plate before placing the rest of the pancakes on Chase's plate.

Ashleigh's eyes slid to Melanie, whose plate was empty. One side of Melanie's mouth tugged downward. Too bad. If Melanie was going to cause Ashleigh trouble, then Melanie could wait to eat.

"Have you eaten yet?" Chase asked Melanie.

Melanie smiled sweetly. "You go ahead, Chase. You'll need your strength to deal with my sister."

A laugh Ashleigh recognized as nervous slipped from Chase's lips.

If Ashleigh had been sitting down, she would have kicked Melanie under the table. As it was, she glared at her sister, then went back to the griddle and poured more batter.

Eventually, they all had enough to eat, including Ashleigh, which was when Melanie excused herself and took Avery down the hall and away from Ashleigh and Chase. Thank goodness.

She and Chase went into the living room where they sat near each other on the couch.

"Now that we're alone," Chase said, which made Ashleigh brace herself for what he was going to say, "will you tell me why you were crying last night?"

She thought about her determination to put the past behind her, but that would never happen until she managed to truly forgive Chase. Gathering herself, she drew in a deep but quiet breath, then she slowly exhaled. "That song? From last night? *Somebody I Used to Know?*"

He looked slightly perplexed. "Yeah?"

"I had in on repeat on my iPod. Six years ago." Would he get what she was trying to say?

A light came on in his eyes. "You mean when I…left."

Now he was catching on. "Yeah."

The memory of him leaving had brought rivers of tears to her eyes? Chase felt like an insensitive jerk. Which he knew he had been, the way he'd left and never looked back. For some reason, at the time he'd left, it had never occurred to him that Ashleigh would be so broken up about him heading out of Emerald Falls to make his way in the world. True, he'd been her boyfriend and they'd been dating for a year, but they'd been so young—she had been twenty and he had been twenty-two. Had she really expected him to stick around forever?

He looked at her face and realized that maybe that was exactly what she'd expected. And he'd done the exact opposite. Did he regret it? The only thing he regretted was causing her so much grief. Still, he knew that his response just then mattered. "I really caused you anguish, didn't I?"

Her jaw tightened like she was trying to hold on to her emotions. Then she nodded. "Yeah, you did." She paused. "You pretty much shattered my heart."

Hearing those words made him feel awful. He'd had no idea that affect his leaving had had on her.

Swallowing over the knot in his throat, he said, "I'm so sorry, Ashleigh. I never meant for you to feel like you didn't matter to me, because you do. I was young and stupid and only thinking about myself and my future."

She nodded, then she stared at him for several long moments before her eyes softened. "I forgive you, Chase."

Though he hadn't known he needed to be forgiven, he could see how much peace it brought her to say those words. "Thank you," he simply said.

CHAPTER 36

*A*shleigh felt as if a boulder had been removed from her heart, one that had kept her from allowing anyone inside. It was cathartic, telling him how much she'd been hurt and knowing he heard her. Now she could truly move on, although the question was, move on to what?

"Can we talk about what happened last night?" Chase asked.

"I thought we just did."

He chuckled in what sounded like embarrassment, then he pulled something out of his pocket. It was the engagement ring.

Ashleigh looked at the sparkling diamond in his palm. "Oh. That."

His smile grew. "Yes. This."

She lifted her gaze from the ring to his face. "Did you tell your mom what happened?"

He shook his head. "No. Not yet." His eyebrows rose as undisguised hope filled his eyes. "Do I need to?"

She understood what he was implying. Would she take back what she'd said and become re-fake-engaged? The idea made her smile.

His lips tugged upward, parting slightly. "What?"

"I don't think you need to tell your mom anything right now."

It was only when his eyes closed and his head bent forward as he exhaled audibly that Ashleigh realized how much this had been burdening him. Knowing her simple yes or no held so much power was a bit overwhelming, but it felt good to know that she'd made a choice that would bring happiness to both him and his mother.

He kept his eyes closed for several seconds as if he was saying a prayer of thanks, which hit her even harder. Had her response been an answer to a prayer?

When Chase lifted his chin and met her gaze, a smile slowly built on his face. "I'd planned a surprise for you, but after last night I wasn't sure if I should go through with it."

Intrigued, she raised her eyebrows. "What is it?"

"I hired Fiona Cunningham, the fashion designer, to bring several wedding gowns for you to try on."

Ashleigh sat up straighter. "Wait." She pointed at the floor. "Here? At my house?" At each word, her eyes grew wider.

Chase laughed. "No. I didn't think you'd want that."

She exhaled in relief. "You're right." Her forehead creased. "Where, then?"

He smiled. "At the Emerald Falls Hotel."

"Oh. When?"

"Any time after lunch. Which I'd like to take you to."

Rather overwhelmed by all he was doing for her, for a moment—maybe more than a moment—she fervently wished this was all for real. Then she put aside her heart's desire and focused on reality—this was all for Sheila and it would be worth it.

She smiled. "Okay. I, uh, can you give me some time to get ready?"

He laughed. "Of course." Then he held out the ring. "Will you put this back on?"

She took it from him and smiled. "Yes." Then she slipped it on her left ring finger.

He got to his feet and she rose as well. As she stood beside him, all she wanted was for him to take her into his arms, but his arms stubbornly stayed at his sides.

Why had the unexpected desire swept over her? But she knew. Despite her best efforts to suppress her love for him, her heart refused to be restrained.

Anxious to think about something else, she led the way to the front door, stopping next to it. "I'll see you in a while."

He stared at her for several beats and she had the absurd thought that he was going to kiss her, but he didn't move.

Finally, he opened the door. "I'll be back at noon." Moments later, he was gone.

Chase should have kissed her. He'd wanted to as they'd stood by the door, but she'd made it clear that there would be no kissing until their wedding day. And even then, it would all be for show. He understood now how badly he'd broken her heart six years earlier and he understood why she wouldn't allow any touching—he didn't like it, but he accepted it.

He drove home, beyond relieved that things had gotten back on track, and when he got home, he found Jordyn in the kitchen making an omelet.

"Hi," he said as he walked in, not able to hide the happiness in his voice.

She sprinkled diced green peppers and grated cheddar cheese on the omelet. "Looks like your talk went well."

"Yep. It's back on." He didn't want to share any details—it was too personal—so he asked, "Mom up yet?"

Jordyn nodded. "She's awake." She gestured with her chin toward the omelet as she flipped it over. "I'm making her breakfast."

"Can I help?"

Smiling, Jordyn said, "Yeah. Will you make buttered toast?"

Glad he could do more than stand and watch, he placed two slices of bread in the toaster. "Coming right up."

Once breakfast was made, Jordyn carried the tray to their mom's room. Chase was right behind her.

"Good morning," Jordyn sang out as she walked through the doorway.

"Oh, thank you." Their mom, who was sitting up in bed, looked at Chase. "To both of you." Her eyes shone. "I have the best children a mother could ask for."

Chase stood at the foot of the bed and shook his head. "You have that backwards, Mom. *We* have the best mother."

She chuckled, then turned her attention to the tray that Jordyn set across her lap. "What did you make?"

Jordyn adjusted the tray. "Omelet, buttered toast, orange juice, and coffee."

She smiled. "Looks delicious." She patted the mattress. "Sit down and visit with me."

Chase moved to the opposite side of the bed from his mom and settled in, leaning against the pillows. He looked at his sister. "Jordyn?"

She laughed. "I need to run a few errands."

That was fine. He was happy for the opportunity to spend one on one time with his mom. They bid Jordyn goodbye.

"How's the wedding planning going?" his mom asked.

Chase thought about all that had transpired since the evening before, then smiled. "Great. Ashleigh's getting her dress today."

Concern washed across her face. "Will there be enough time to get it altered?"

He chuckled. "Should be. I hired a designer to get the job done."

His mom put a hand on his arm. "Oh, Chase. You're going to be such a good husband."

That hit him hard, because he wasn't going to be a husband at all. In fact, he'd been looking for the right person to pose as the officiator to pretend to marry them. An actor who looked the part and would be convincing. And since he had to do it on the down-low, it wasn't as easy as he'd thought it would be. But he'd get it done.

He and his mom chatted about the wedding and childhood memories and Chase's business. It wasn't until it was time for him to get ready for his lunch date with Ashleigh that he realized his mom had set her food tray on the bedside table, her food barely touched.

"Aren't you hungry?" he asked.

"Not really." Her eyebrows gathered in as she sighed heavily. "I'm sorry, Chase. I know you and Jordyn spent time making it for me."

"No, it's fine. I'm just...I'm worried about you."

Sadness was etched in her eyes. "I'll be honest, son. I'm not feeling very well today."

Alarmed, he said, "Should I call the hospice nurse?"

She shook her head and exhaled audibly. "No. I just...I need to sleep." She smiled, but her eyes showed utter exhaustion. "Go now. Be with Ashleigh." She scooted down and pulled the covers up.

Chase pressed a gentle kiss to her forehead. "I'll be back soon to check on you."

She nodded but didn't open her eyes.

Chase took the tray from the bedside table and left the room, his eyes filling with tears. His heart was full—of sadness for his mom and of gratitude toward Ashleigh for choosing to bring the gift of happiness to his mom despite what he'd put her through.

CHAPTER 37

*W*hen Ashleigh answered the door at noon, she could see that Chase was upset. His brow was wrinkled and he didn't even smile when he saw her.

She held the door open wider for him to enter. "What's wrong?"

He shook his head as he walked inside, then he stopped and faced her, scrubbing his face with his hands. When his hands dropped to his side, he frowned. "It's my mom. She's not..." He shook his head. "She's getting worse." He choked up on that last bit.

Ashleigh didn't even think, she just wrapped her arms around his waist and laid her head against his chest. His arms went around her and he held her tight, tighter than she'd been held for a long, long time.

His body shook as he quietly wept.

Remembering the loss of her own parents, she felt tears fill her own eyes as she clung to him.

Glad she could offer some comfort, when he finally drew away, wiping his eyes, she had an overwhelming craving to have him hold her again. But she wanted it to have nothing to do with grief and everything to do with him loving her.

This was too hard, this back and forth, this love him but not let herself feel it, this pretending to be in love when she really was but she wasn't able to act on it. If the situation with Sheila wasn't so grave, Ashleigh would have no choice but to end this. But she couldn't do that. Not now.

"Can I get you something?" she asked Chase, her voice soft.

He shook his head and softly chuckled. "Sorry I'm being such a baby."

His mother was *dying*. If that didn't make him break down, what would? She lowered her chin and stared at him. "Chase. Come on."

He smiled, his eyes soft. "Thank you, Ashleigh. For what you're doing. It means..." He shook his head. "It means *everything* to my mom."

What about to you? she wanted to ask but didn't dare. She'd barely forgiven him that very day. She wasn't about to make this awkward for both of them. She was there to do a job and she was going to do it.

"Are you hungry?" he asked, clearly ready to move on to something else.

She nodded. "Yep. And afterwards Melanie, Jordyn, and Taylor are going to meet me at the hotel to help me pick a dress."

He smiled. "Great."

They walked out the door and got in his Lamborghini. When they reached the Emerald Falls Hotel a short time later, they went into the restaurant together, and after they ordered, Ashleigh couldn't help but be excited about what would come after their lunch date.

"Tell me about the appointment with Fiona Cunningham," she asked. "I mean, how much time do I have to try on dresses?"

A smile slowly spread across his face. "As much time as you need. I hired her for the day. She's getting everything set up for you and your bridesmaids."

It was like a fairytale—small-town librarian swept away by a dashing billionaire who lays the world at her feet. Except for the part where they were madly in love.

Guess she couldn't have the *whole* fairytale.

Putting on a brave smile—which wasn't too hard when she shoved down the feelings of unrequited love and focused on the fairytale part that the world would see—she said, "That's amazing, Chase. Thank you."

"Of course." He laughed. "Gotta make sure you have a proper dress for our Christmas wedding."

Why did he have to say that so casually? Did he really feel so clinical about the whole thing?

※

It was hard to pretend that this meant nothing when his feelings for Ashleigh were growing stronger by the day. Especially when he thought about the way she'd embraced him when he'd lost it earlier. It had felt amazing to have her comfort him when he was feeling so down, but underneath that, it had felt so right to have her in his arms again. In fact, the moment his arms had gone around her, the familiarity of her body pressing against his had washed over him. Holding her was like coming home.

"What are you thinking about?" she asked.

He realized he was smiling while staring just past her shoulder. Caught thinking about her, he chuckled as he shifted his eyes to hers. "Truthfully?"

Her head tilted. "That would be nice."

That drew another laugh out of him. "I was thinking about how comfortable it felt when you hugged me earlier."

Her eyebrows shot up. Guess she hadn't expected him to be *that* truthful.

She straightened her napkin on her lap. "Oh."

The server set their food in front of them, giving them both a brief moment of distraction.

CHAPTER 38

Knowing Chase was thinking about their embrace earlier sent a thrill of excitement through Ashleigh. She knew it didn't mean as much to him as it had meant to her, but just knowing it was on his mind gave her an unexpected jolt of...hope?

Hope for what, though?

Confused, she lifted her fork and stabbed a chunk of cucumber.

"Now it's my turn to ask you," Chase said, "what are *you* thinking about?"

She lifted her gaze and looked at his earnest expression. Should she be honest? Before she could let an internal debate begin, she said, "I still care about you, Chase." Such an understatement, but he had to get an inkling of what was going on in her heart.

His expression softened. "I care about you too."

Okay. That was nice. But what did it really mean? Because she knew what *she* meant—she was still in love with him. Head over heels. Had he ever been in love with her?

No. He couldn't have been. If he had, he wouldn't have left her the way he did.

Dropping her gaze back to her plate, she struggled to soothe her aching heart.

"What's wrong?" he asked, his voice soft.

She was so over pretending. With determination, she met his beseeching eyes. "Did you ever love me?"

He stared back.

Ashleigh's heart pounded as she waited to hear his answer.

Chase was completely caught off guard by Ashleigh's question. *Had* he ever loved her? He'd cared for her deeply back then. Love though? He wasn't sure. But that was then. Now, his feelings were growing. Rapidly. It kind of shocked him to realize how quickly he was falling for her. Developing deep feelings for her wasn't what he'd bargained for. This was supposed to be all about granting his mom's dying wish, not falling in love with a former girlfriend. Still, there it was.

Wait. Was he falling in love with her?

He looked at those blue, blue eyes, that sweet, vulnerable face, thought about how unselfish she was, how kind and caring. If he paid attention to what his heart was telling him, he would have to admit that he was definitely falling in love with her.

Still, he wasn't ready to admit it. It was so unexpected and it was completely new. Anyway, she'd asked about how he'd felt back then. "I've always cared for you, Ashleigh."

She stared at him a moment, then sighed and shook her head. "Let's talk about something else."

Eager to agree, he nodded. "Yes."

They moved to other topics as they ate, much to Chase's relief, and when the meal was done, he escorted her through the lobby and to the elevator. "I'll bring you to the room where Fiona Cunningham is waiting, but I'm not going to stick around. I mean, even though this is pretend, I still shouldn't see the dress before the big day."

She smiled. "True."

When they reached the room, Chase knocked. A moment later a young woman answered. Chase introduced himself and Ashleigh. The woman smiled. "I'm Ruby, Fiona's assistant." She held the door open and looked at Ashleigh. "We're ready for you."

"That's my cue to say goodbye," Chase said as his eyes went to Ashleigh's face. He could see a mix of emotions there —excitement and melancholy among them. "Do you want me to pick you up when you're done?"

She shook her head. "I'll get a ride from Melanie."

Disappointed, he smiled. "Okay. I'll choose a band and let Deena know which one to hire."

She nodded, then stepped into the room. As she went inside, Chase caught a glimpse of racks of wedding gowns. The sight sent an unexpected wave of longing cascading over him—a longing for a real relationship with Ashleigh.

If he could really marry her, would he?

To his utter shock, the answer was yes.

Stunned, he turned and made his way unsteadily down the hall.

CHAPTER 39

An enormous array of white wedding gowns hung on racks in the spacious suite. Another rack held gowns in reds and greens—obviously for Ashleigh's bridesmaids. A platform sat in the middle of the room with a huge three-way mirror in front of it.

Ashleigh was overwhelmed. All of this was for her? Then again, Chase was extremely wealthy. Even though the wedding was fake, Chase was obviously doing all he could to make this nice for her.

"Good afternoon," a woman in her forties said to Ashleigh as she walked toward her with a smile. Her hair was cut in a short, stylish manner, and she wore a pair of gray slacks with a cranberry-colored sweater. She held out her hand, which Ashleigh took. "I'm Fiona. It is so good to meet you."

Ashleigh smiled, Fiona's sincerity putting her at ease. "It's good to meet you, Fiona. I'm Ashleigh."

Fiona released her hand, then swept her gaze down Ashleigh's body. "You have a fabulous figure. It won't be hard to find the perfect dress."

Flattered, Ashleigh felt her cheeks warm, but she had an important concern. "The wedding is in eleven days. Is there really enough time to get a dress fitted?"

Fiona laughed. "Of course, my dear."

Relieved, Ashleigh smiled. "Great."

"Now, let's talk about the style you have in mind. Fit and flair? A-line?"

Ashleigh had no idea. "Uh, maybe you can help me figure out what would look best?"

Smiling broadly, Fiona said, "Of course."

A knock sounded on the hotel door. Ashleigh watched as Ruby hurried to answer it. A moment later, Melanie walked in.

"My maid of honor!" Ashleigh exclaimed, thrilled to have her sister there.

"You didn't start without me, did you?" Melanie asked with a smile as she gave Ashleigh a hug. Ashleigh had already prepped her to pretend this was all real. Although Jordyn knew the truth, Taylor didn't. Neither did Fiona and Ruby.

Ashleigh smiled. "We were just about to begin."

Jordyn and Taylor arrived a few moments later. After Ashleigh introduced her bridesmaids to Fiona and Ruby, Fiona selected several dresses for Ashleigh to try on.

Ashleigh followed Fiona into an adjoining bedroom. Fiona closed the door, then helped Ashleigh change into the first gown. A full-length mirror allowed Ashleigh to see if the dress was a contender before showing it to the others.

"What do you think?" Fiona asked as she stood beside Ashleigh.

Ashleigh stared at her reflection, stunned at how absolutely gorgeous the dress was. It was a V-neck ball gown with a beaded lace appliquéd bodice, but at the waist it turned into frothy layers of white tulle. It was as if Ashleigh was floating on a cloud.

"I love it," she breathed. But it was only the first dress of many, so she couldn't choose it just yet. "Let's see what the others think."

Fiona nodded briskly, going to the bedroom door and opening it to allow Ashleigh to walk into the main space of the suite. The moment she entered, gasps were heard all around. They liked it too. Not able to suppress her smile, Ashleigh stepped onto the platform and looked at the dress from all angles. It was lovely and perfect.

Ashleigh turned around to see the faces of her bridesmaids. All seemed to be in agreement that this one was stunning.

"You should try on some others," Melanie said with a smile that seemed forced, "just to be sure this is the one you love."

Ashleigh nodded, but before she left the platform, she turned and gazed at herself in the mirror. She imagined walking down the aisle toward Chase. When he saw her, his eyes would light up with love and adoration, and when she reached him, he would take her hand and say his vows, making her his wife.

Caught up in the moment, her heart sang with joy. But when she remembered it was fake, the joy crashed into a sharp ache that made her heart hurt. Her radiant smile dimmed and she turned away from the mirror.

As she stepped down, she caught Melanie's eye. Maybe Melanie could see the sadness in Ashleigh's face, or maybe Melanie was having her own issues with the charade, but Melanie's lips were pressed together in a slight grimace.

Wanting to cheer herself up as much as her sister, Ashleigh put on a radiant smile. Melanie smiled in return, but Ashleigh knew it didn't reflect her true feelings.

Ashleigh tried on several more dresses, but the consensus was unanimous, the first one was The One. Ecstatic that she'd found such a gorgeous dress, as Fiona pinned it at the waist and hem to make it fit perfectly, Ashleigh kept her focus on how truly happy Sheila would be. Of course she wanted to be happy herself, but this wasn't about her and it wasn't about Chase. It was about Sheila. As long as she kept that front and center in her mind, everything would be okay.

CHAPTER 40

"What's wrong?" Ashleigh heard Jordyn ask Melanie as they looked through the bridesmaid's dresses.

Trying to pretend like she couldn't hear them, Ashleigh kept her focus on the dresses she was looking through. Taylor was nearby pulling out dresses she liked—too far to hear the conversation.

"Are you really okay with this?" Melanie asked Jordyn.

"It *is* for a good cause." Jordyn spoke just above a whisper. Ashleigh had to strain to hear. "But I'll be honest. If it was for real, I wouldn't be happy."

"What? Why not?" Annoyance was clear in Melanie's tone.

Ashleigh had to subdue a laugh. Her sister had been glad when Ashleigh had told her she'd given Chase the ring back.

Suddenly Melanie was offended because Jordyn didn't like the idea of her brother marrying Ashleigh? Even so, she was glad her sister was sticking up for her.

"You don't think Chase should marry my sister?"

"I just...I don't know if her intentions would be pure."

"Pure?" Melanie asked. "What does *that* mean?"

Resisting the urge to step into the conversation, Ashleigh listened from eight feet away, although she moved a little closer to make sure she didn't miss anything.

"My brother's a very successful man. A very *wealthy* man. A lot of women would love to get their hands on his money."

Ashleigh turned her head far enough to see the two women out of the corner of her eye.

Melanie shook her head. "That's not my sister. She doesn't care about money." She paused a beat. "Maybe you forgot that *your brother* broke her heart. She really loved him, you know."

"That was a long time ago. Things change, you know?" Jordyn took a dress off the rack. "I have to protect him from...well, from predators."

"My sister is not a predator." It came out as a whisper-scream.

Okay, time to stop this. Acting like she was oblivious to the conversation, Ashleigh stepped over to them. "Find any dresses you like?"

Jordyn looked at her with a guilty face, but Melanie looked angry.

Ashleigh understood how Melanie felt, but she wasn't

upset. She was no predator—she'd loved Chase before he'd even started his business. Yes, having money was nice, but it was Chase that she loved. Even if he didn't love her back.

Jordyn held up a pretty green dress. "This one looks nice."

Tempted to choose a different one just to spite her, instead Ashleigh fingered the dress and smiled. "I think it would look good on you." She turned to Melanie. "What do you think, Mel?"

Melanie frowned. "I really don't care."

"What about this one?" Taylor asked, carrying over a red dress. She was probably the happiest member of the bridal party. To her, the Christmas wedding was so romantic. Ashleigh wished *she* could feel the same excitement.

Shoving down her misgivings, she smiled at Taylor. "I like that one too."

Fiona had all three bridesmaids try on both the green and red dresses in different styles. In the end, they all agreed that the red looked the best with Ashleigh's wedding gown, although each bridesmaid wore a slightly different style dress, just in the same red fabric.

It was coming together nicely.

"We will have a fitting on Wednesday," Fiona said. "One week before the wedding.

After the appointment was made, and Ashleigh thanked everyone for coming, she and Melanie drove home. Melanie didn't mention the conversation she'd had with Jordyn, so Ashleigh didn't say anything either. It was enough to know how Jordyn really felt and to know that Melanie had stood up for her.

"When are you seeing Chase again?" Melanie asked as she turned onto their street.

"I don't know. We didn't schedule anything. Anyway, I think he wants to spend time with his mom. It sounds like she's not doing well."

"That's so sad."

"I know." She didn't want to tell her sister how Chase had cried earlier that day. "It takes me back to when we lost Mom and Dad in the car accident."

Melanie pulled into the driveway. "Yeah. That was the hardest thing I've ever gone through."

"I know. Thank goodness we had Grandma to take us in." Ashleigh didn't know what was worse—having weeks to dread the loss of your parent but be able to say goodbye, or losing your parent without warning but not have the dread leading up to it. Any way you sliced it, it was awful to go through. She was glad she could be there for Chase. She just wished it hadn't taken something so sad to bring him back into her life.

CHAPTER 41

*A*shleigh had been on Chase's mind all afternoon. How were things going with Fiona? Had she found a dress? Was it all too much and she was going to call it off again? The suspense was killing him. Still, he wanted to give her some space, so he waited until the next morning to text her. *Good morning. How did it go yesterday with Fiona Cunningham?*

She replied a few minutes later. *Great! Found a dress for me and the bridesmaids, so I'd call it a success.*

That's great news!

Sounded like she was still going through with the wedding.

Chase wanted to see her. After he'd listened to the bands the previous afternoon and told Deena which one to hire, he'd spent the balance of the day with his mom, which had been wonderful—he'd even managed to forget she was sick for a while. But the entire time, Ashleigh had been on his mind. His mom had even commented on it, saying that she could tell how much he loved Ashleigh. The comment had startled him. Because he wasn't in love with her, right? That is, he felt like he was falling in love with her, but it was a new thing for him.

Or was his mom right and he'd been in love with her all along and hadn't even realized it or hadn't let himself feel it until now? Until he was ready?

It didn't matter. The only thing he knew was that the more he thought about her, the more he wanted to be with her.

He texted her. *How would you like to go bowling tonight?*

She replied with a bowling emoji. *Sounds good.*

Great! I'll pick you up at six.

After that, he spent the rest of the day working on his laptop and trying not to think about her, but when it was time to leave, he logged off his computer faster than he had in years.

A short time later, as he stood on her porch waiting for her to answer his knock, he couldn't stop his brain from picturing her in a wedding gown as she glided down the aisle toward him. She would be radiant, her eyes focused only on him. And he would be waiting to take her hand in his and make her his wife.

The door swung open. It was Melanie, who frowned when she saw him. "Hi."

His daydream pierced, he smiled at her despite her less than warm greeting. "Hello."

She sighed, then opened the door to allow him to enter. "Ashleigh will be out in a few minutes."

"Thanks."

She turned and walked away.

"Sorry to keep you waiting," Ashleigh said as she came into the room a few minutes later, her face bright and cheerful—such a contrast to her sister.

Chase stared at her, his chest growing warm at the sight of her. It seemed she nearly always wore a smile. And those eyes—sparkling blue like the crystal clear waters of the Caribbean. Then there was her bubbly personality and the way she seemed to always think of the needs of others before her own.

She was the perfect woman.

And he'd let her go.

The truth of it hit him right between the eyes.

He had been an idiot to walk away from her six years earlier, and now she didn't trust him with her heart. Not that he blamed her, but was it possible to change her mind? He didn't know, but all of a sudden he had the overwhelming desire to gain her trust. And her love. He also wouldn't mind drawing her into his arms and kissing her until she melted against him.

"Did you pick a band?" she asked, yanking him out of his fantasy.

"Uh, yeah. It's all taken care of."

"Great." She stared at him like she was waiting for him to do something.

"Oh, uh, ready to go?"

She laughed. "Yeah."

They went out to his Lamborghini. He opened the passenger door for her and helped her in. On the way to the bowling alley, Chase couldn't help but glance at her from time to time.

"What?" she asked with a perplexed look.

He laughed. "Just glad you're here."

She gave him a look he couldn't read.

Was Chase playing with her? They were going out because they had to keep up appearances. Nothing more. Well, maybe because they enjoyed each other's company. But he didn't have to say things like that. It just confused the situation.

At the bowling alley, as they took turns knocking down the pins, Ashleigh found herself having a great time. Keeping things platonic helped tremendously. At least when she convinced herself that all she needed from him was friendship. Her heart knew that was a lie, but she managed to tamp down those feelings enough to have a good time.

At the end of their date, Chase asked if she would go out with him the next night. Somewhat reluctantly, she agreed.

Over the rest of the week they went out several times. As

much as Ashleigh enjoyed spending time with Chase, it only made her love him more. It was almost too much to bear.

She and her bridesmaids also had a fitting with Fiona. A final fitting was scheduled for the Monday before the wedding.

On Saturday morning, four days before the wedding, Ashleigh woke to a text from Chase asking her if she wanted to go to the karaoke restaurant that night. Her heart immediately yearned to be with him, but her head told her to be careful.

Her heart won out and she agreed to the date.

CHAPTER 42

*D*espite the sadness of dealing with his mom's illness, Chase was having a good month—being with Ashleigh nearly so much over the previous two weeks had been more wonderful than he could ever have imagined. Now, as they drove to the karaoke restaurant, he couldn't hold back his smile.

The restaurant was a lot more crowded than it had been the last time they'd been there, but that was fine. More of a party atmosphere. A man was belting out a Christmas song on the stage. Chase looked at Ashleigh. She seemed to glow from within. Not able to stop himself, he took her hand in his. She gave him a sharp look, but she didn't yank her hand away. Thrilled that she was letting him do that much, he led her to a small table. He released her hand and pulled out a chair for her. She smiled at him before sitting.

Wanting to be close to her, he sat in the adjoining chair. "Do you want to eat before we perform?"

She chuckled. "Yes, that's a good idea."

They placed their orders and watched as a woman got on stage and began singing. It was all background noise to Chase, whose only interest was in being with Ashleigh. He scooted his chair closer to hers so they could both be comfortable while watching the performances.

He thought about the songs they'd sung the last time they'd been there. "Do you want to sing Christmas songs again?"

With less than two feet between them, when Ashleigh swiveled her head to look at him, Chase had to work to not close that space and kiss her.

"Yes," she said in answer to his question. "I'd love to sing Christmas songs again." She smiled. "But I'll pick them this time."

He tilted his head. "You didn't like the ones we did before?"

She grimaced. "Didn't they feel a bit, I don't know, intimate?"

He wanted to feel intimate with her, but he didn't want her to feel uncomfortable. "I'll sing whatever you pick."

Her eyebrows rose. "Oh, really?"

"As long as you don't make me look like a fool."

She laughed.

The server set their food on the table. They chatted as

they ate, and once they were done, Ashleigh turned to him with raised eyebrows. "Ready to sing?"

As long as she was involved, he would do anything. "Yep."

They stood and made their way to the stage.

Kind of excited to perform with Chase, Ashleigh scanned through the catalog of Christmas songs. She told the music guy which ones she wanted, then she and Chase got on stage.

Have Yourself A Merry Little Christmas started playing. Ashleigh looked at Chase and smiled, and when he smiled back, her heart did a little flip. She liked the way he'd taken her hand when they'd gotten there, although she didn't know if it had been a spontaneous gesture or if it had been a calculated move because they were supposed to be engaged.

Hoping it was the former, she focused on the words on the screen, letting the music fill her soul. She adored Christmas carols. Next, *Let it Snow! Let it Snow! Let it Snow!* came on. After that they sang *Silver Bells* then *White Christmas*.

When it looked like someone else wanted a turn, Ashleigh reluctantly told the music guy that they were done.

The audience applauded. Ashleigh was about to get off the stage when someone shouted, "Don't forget the kiss!"

Wait. Had she misheard? She looked in the direction the voice had come from. "What?"

Several people pointed to the area above her and Chase's head and shouted, "Mistletoe! Mistletoe!"

Ashleigh tipped her head back. Sure enough, there was a large sprig of mistletoe hanging right above the stage. That hadn't been there the last time. She looked at Chase, who seemed like was suppressing a laugh. He *wanted* to kiss her, the brat. To be honest, kissing him didn't sound like the worst thing in the world. As long as she knew it was for fun, for pretend. Yeah, that would make it okay.

As she stared at Chase, one of his eyebrows arched like he was asking *Are we gonna do this?*

With the crowd watching, Ashleigh really didn't have a choice. Besides, they were supposed be crazy for each other and days away from their wedding. Anyway, what was one little kiss?

Shoving a smile onto her lips, she tilted her chin up and locked eyes with Chase. Now both of his eyebrows got into the act, rising upward like he was asking if she was sure. Her eyes widened like *Just do this already.*

His face relaxed as a smile slowly curved his lips, then one of his fingers went under her chin. His touch sent a current of electricity surging through her and their mouths hadn't even gotten involved yet.

Uh-oh. She was in trouble.

"Ashleigh," he whispered as his eyes stayed steady on hers. Then, ever so slowly, his lips moved closer, ever closer. It was completely tantalizing. He was taking so long Ashleigh didn't think she could take it a second longer.

Finally, mercifully, his mouth reached hers. Her heart sang with joy as the familiar feel of his lips touching hers raced through her. Then, as if on instinct, she wound her arms around his neck, pulling him in tight. His arms went around her waist, holding her against him.

Wow! Just, wow! She'd forgotten what a good kisser he was. Or maybe she'd blocked it to keep from missing him so desperately when he'd left.

That's right. He'd left. And he would again.

Heart sinking now, Ashleigh unwound her arms from around his neck and gently pushed him away.

He released her as well and took a step back, his eyes on her.

The sound of the crowd whooping and hollering was somewhere in the background. All Ashleigh could think about was the ache in her heart. Chase Matthews was the only man she'd ever loved. She hadn't gotten over him after six years and she never would.

Tears filled her eyes. Mortified, she turned away and nearly stumbled off of the stage.

That kiss. It was better than anything Chase could have imagined. And it wasn't like he hadn't kissed her before—they'd kissed plenty back in the day. But something about this kiss was different. And he knew what it was. His brain had finally caught up with his heart. He was in love with her.

Totally and completely. Maybe he always had been, but he'd been too focused on his career to notice.

When she'd stared at him after they'd stopped kissing, her eyes had had a haunted look before tears had filled them, and a moment later she'd turned away and had left the stage, somewhat unsteadily.

Chase went after her, the sound of the cheering crowd fading as his focus was one hundred percent on Ashleigh. She went straight to their table, scooped up her coat and purse, then made a beeline to the exit.

"Wait!" he shouted, but his voice was drowned out by the noise of the full restaurant and the song that was blaring over the speakers as someone took the stage.

He reached the exit a few moments after she went through it, but she had already disappeared.

CHAPTER 43

Crouching next to a car in the parking lot, Ashleigh could see Chase looking for her. She felt ridiculous hiding from him, but she needed a minute. She had to think. The realization that she was desperately in love with him and always would be had thrown her for a loop. It was like the song they'd sung at their first karaoke night, *Baby, It's Cold Outside*. She kept trying to pull away and he kept bringing her back and she wanted him to bring her back, but then again she didn't. And now she was hunkered down next to a car hiding from him. If it wasn't so sad it would be ridiculous.

"Ashleigh," he called out, his head turning from side to side as he scanned the lot. "Ashleigh, are you out here?"

Hearing him calling for her only made her feel worse. Tears filled her eyes and overflowed her lashes. Furiously wiping them away, she peered through the windows on the car she was hiding beside. She could see Chase looking in all directions, then he stopped and pulled out his phone before tapping something in.

Ashleigh's phone vibrated in her purse. She took it out and read the message: *Are you okay? Where are you?*

Knowing that if she didn't want to talk to him face to face she would have to reassure him that she was all right, she tapped in a message. *I'm fine.*

She watched as he read the message, then he tapped in a reply: *Where are you? Did you go back inside?*

Dang it. Why wouldn't he just leave her to her pity party?

Quieting her sigh, she replied. *I took a Lyft home.*

She could see his puzzled expression, like he was wondering how she'd gotten away so fast and why she'd left without saying goodbye. Resisting the urge to say anything further, she stayed hidden. Finally, Chase got into his car and drove away.

When he was out of sight, Ashleigh stood and looked around. Luckily, no one had seen her weird behavior. She took a moment to get her emotions under control before she arranged to have a Lyft pick her up.

As the Lyft drove her home, guilt at the way she'd treated Chase sliced through her. She'd forgiven him for what he'd done to her, so there was no holding that against him. It was all on her now, the way she was acting.

The Lyft pulled up to her house. Half-afraid Chase would be parked there waiting for her, when she didn't see his Lamborghini, she breathed a sigh of relief, then went inside.

"Hi, there," Melanie said when Ashleigh walked in. She was reading a book to Avery.

"Hey."

Glad her sister was occupied, Ashleigh went into the kitchen, set her purse on the counter, and began making a mug of hot cocoa. By the time it was ready to drink, Melanie had joined her.

"How was your date?"

Turning to her sister with a grimace, Ashleigh said, "I ran out on him."

"What?"

Ashleigh blew across the top of her hot cocoa. "Yep. I'm sure he's completely confused right about now." She took a sip. *Aw. Perfect.*

"I'm confused too. I mean, why'd you run out?"

The despair she'd felt when she'd realized how much she loved him but that they would never be together washed over her again and tears made a second appearance. She set her mug down and dabbed at her eyes. "Because I love him."

Melanie stared at her. "That didn't clear up anything."

"I know," she said as tears filled her voice. "It's just, I love him so much. But for him this is all fake." The tears were really falling now. Annoyed with herself but not able to get it together, Ashleigh grabbed a tissue and blew her nose. It didn't help. She took a deep, steadying breath, which helped a little.

Melanie looked at her with a mix of pity and an *I told you so.*

"I know," Ashleigh cried. "You were right. Agreeing to be fake-engaged was a big mistake."

Melanie's lips pursed like she was trying not to look triumphant.

Oddly grateful for her sister's reaction as it replaced her despair with irritation, Ashleigh finally managed to slow her tears.

"I'm sorry, Ash. I didn't want to be right."

Ashleigh heard her phone vibrating in her purse. It kept going. It was a phone call. She dug her phone out. It was Chase. She swiped to reject the call. Several moments later a text arrived. *I need to talk to you.*

She showed Melanie the text.

"What are you going to do?"

Ashleigh set her phone on the counter. "I don't know. I mean, I'll still do the stupid wedding, but I can't face him."

"You can't just ignore him."

"Why not?"

Melanie tilted her head like *Come on, Ash. You know that's not realistic.* Then she frowned as she straightened. "Do what you want. It's not like you'll listen to me anyway."

That was true.

Melanie walked out of the kitchen. Ashleigh picked up her mug of hot cocoa and her phone and went into her bedroom. She set the mug on her bedside table, then flopped onto the bed with her phone still in her hand. She pulled up

Chase's social media account and scrolled through all the pictures of him, which didn't help her feel any better.

Her phone vibrated in her hand, startling her. It was another text from Chase. *What's going on? Why won't you talk to me?*

A moment later another text arrived. *Was it the kiss?*

Then another. *I'm sorry I kissed you.*

The memory of their kiss filled her mind and her heart. Being held in Chase's arms had felt so good and so right, and his kiss...heavenly. A kiss seasoned with her love for him had no choice but to be wonderful.

Deciding to give him the courtesy of a reply, she sent him a message. *I just need some space.*

His reply came a few moments later. *OK.*

CHAPTER 44

*C*hase was so confused. He thought Ashleigh had enjoyed that kiss as much as he had, but then she'd run out and left him, finding her own way home. And now she said she needed space. Space for what, though?

Trying not to worry too much about it, he worked on his laptop for a while, then went to bed.

The next morning, Sunday, the first thing he did was check his phone for new messages. None were from Ashleigh. He stared at her last text. *I just need some space.* Tempted to send her a message, he held off and turned his attention to work, then spent a good chunk of the afternoon with his mom.

Monday started off without any word from Ashleigh. Not happy about it, Chase did manage to complete one important task. He hired an actor to play officiator at the wedding.

As the day went on, his worry meter kicked on. The wedding was supposed to happen in two days, yet he hadn't heard a single thing from Ashleigh. For all he knew, she'd fled Emerald Falls with no intention of showing up to their fake wedding.

He had to talk to her.

He knew she was scheduled to meet with Fiona Cunningham at the Emerald Falls Hotel for a fitting that evening—assuming Ashleigh was still in town. Maybe he could casually appear, just to see her. Only for a second. She might be upset with him, but he had to do it.

"That looks gorgeous," Taylor said as Ashleigh stood on the platform in the hotel room wearing her wedding gown. Melanie and Jordyn were there as well.

Fiona appraised Ashleigh critically, a finger tapping her chin. She lifted her eyes to Ashleigh. "It is perfect, no?"

Staring at her reflection in the three-way mirror, Ashleigh couldn't be more pleased with the way the gown had turned out. It fit her perfectly, and with the tiara and veil atop her head, the look was exquisite. Too bad the thought of seeing Chase again dampened her enthusiasm.

"I love it," she said to Fiona with a smile, then she cut her eyes to Melanie, whose lips were pursed in disapproval. Jordyn didn't look thrilled either, so Ashleigh focused on Taylor, who had enough excitement for all of them.

"Chase is going to be blown away when he sees you walking down the aisle," Taylor gushed.

The mention of Chase and the wedding tore the smile from Ashleigh's lips, but when she saw confusion on Taylor's face, Ashleigh shoved the smile back on.

Ruby, Fiona's assistant, went with Ashleigh into the adjoining bedroom, then helped her take the gown off. "We'll press the gown before we deliver it to your house. You will receive it by tomorrow evening."

The way they'd gotten everything done so quickly amazed Ashleigh, although she understood that Chase's money had helped to grease the wheels. "Thank you so much."

When she went back in the main part of the suite, she watched as Fiona focused on Melanie, Jordyn, and Taylor, making sure their dresses fit perfectly as well.

Touched that these three women were doing this for her —especially Melanie—Ashleigh smiled softly at them. "Thank you for being my bridesmaids." The moment the words left her mouth, it felt disingenuous. The wedding was fake. It was all fake. Even so, Melanie returned her smile. Jordyn, on the other hand, barely looked at her. She wanted to shout *This was your brother's idea and we're doing it for your mother! I don't even want to do it!* Instead, she again focused on Taylor, who looked delighted to be part of such an exciting event. Thank goodness for her friend.

When they were done with the fitting, Jordyn hurried toward the door to leave.

"Wait," Ashleigh called out. Jordyn opened the door but stopped and faced Ashleigh. Not wanting to make a scene, Ashleigh went over to her and spoke quietly. "What's wrong?"

Jordyn huffed a sigh. "I should be asking you that. I mean, what is going on between you and Chase?"

Evidently Chase hadn't told Jordyn anything. But what was happening at home that had Jordyn so riled up? "What do you mean?"

Jordyn gave her a look like *Don't play dumb.* "He just seems really agitated and upset." She narrowed her eyes. "What did you do?"

"What did *I* do?" She couldn't help the annoyance from flying out of her mouth. Compressing her lips, she shook her head. "I didn't do anything, okay? Anyway, we'll figure it out." That was still in question, but it wasn't Jordyn's business. Then it hit her. Chase was upset and agitated? Why?

Then she knew. He was worried she wasn't going to go through with the wedding. She frowned at Jordyn. "You can tell him I'm not backing out."

Jordyn made a scoffing sound. "You can tell him yourself." Then she left the suite, closing the door behind her.

Ashleigh stared at the closed door, her heart hammering in her chest. This was such a mess.

"Everything okay?" Taylor asked from beside her.

Putting on her game face, Ashleigh turned and smiled at her friend. "Yeah."

"Good." She smiled. "I've gotta go, but I'll see you on the

big day." Her eyes twinkled. "Just two more days and you'll be Mrs. Chase Matthews."

Every word Taylor uttered was a twist of the knife in Ashleigh's heart. "Yep," she croaked out.

Taylor squinted at her like she thought Ashleigh was having some sort of attack.

Forcing a fake smile onto her lips—something she was getting really good at—Ashleigh gave her a hug. "See you Wednesday."

Taylor's expression smoothed out. "Bye."

After she left, Ashleigh thanked Fiona and Ruby for all they'd done, then she and Melanie left the suite.

As they waited for the elevator to arrive, Melanie asked Ashleigh what Jordyn had said.

Ashleigh repeated the conversation.

"I'm sure she's got a lot on her plate with her mom so sick and everything."

Momentarily silenced as she remembered why she was going through everything, Ashleigh said a silent prayer on Sheila's behalf.

On the elevator ride down, Ashleigh turned to Melanie. "I really appreciate your support in this..." She sighed audibly. "This wedding."

Melanie gazed at her. "How are you feeling? About Chase and...well, everything?"

Ashleigh shook her head. "I don't know. I mean, I miss him, but seeing him just hurts too much."

Melanie placed her hand on Ashleigh's arm and softly smiled. "You'll get through this."

Not sure that she believed that, Ashleigh nodded anyway.

A moment later, the elevator doors silently slid open and Ashleigh and Melanie walked into the spacious lobby. Ready to go home and bury herself in her to-be-read pile of books, at first Ashleigh didn't notice the man standing up from a chair, but when she heard Melanie's soft intake of breath, she saw the man who owned her heart.

Eyes widening, Ashleigh tried to slow her racing pulse. "Chase. What…what are you doing here?"

"Hi, Ashleigh." He walked over to her and Melanie.

Ashleigh glanced at Melanie, who had a look on her face like *Do you want me to stay?* Not sure what she wanted, she gave no signal to her sister.

"I'll just wait over there," Melanie said as she pointed toward a cluster of empty chairs.

Nodding, Ashleigh kept her focus on Chase, whose eyes were studying her.

"I've been waiting for you to reach out," he said, then he smiled that smile that got her every single time. "I'm done waiting."

The way he said it, like he wasn't willing to wait another second to see her, woke a swarm of butterflies in her belly, sending them swooping. "I…" What was she supposed to say? That she loved him so much she couldn't take being around him?

"Have dinner with me," he said, his tone insistent.

Seeing him had taking her by surprise. She had been completely unprepared. Sitting across from him was out of the question. She shook her head. "I can't. Not... not tonight."

"Okay. What about tomorrow?"

Tomorrow was Christmas Eve. The night before their wedding. It was time to face her feelings, to face him. Nodding, she said, "Yes. Tomorrow."

A smile slowly curved his lips. "Okay. Tomorrow. I'll pick you up at six."

With her focus completely on him, Ashleigh nodded. At that, he turned and strode away.

"What did he say?" Melanie asked as she appeared beside Ashleigh.

Turning to her sister, she knew her face betrayed her feelings. "He's taking me to dinner tomorrow night."

Melanie's eyebrows rose. "You seem pretty happy about that."

To her surprise and dismay, she knew Melanie was right. Despite knowing he would crush her heart, she was eager to spend the evening with him.

CHAPTER 45

*C*hase was thrilled that Ashleigh had agreed to have dinner with him, and as he waited for her to answer her door, he analyzed his feelings. Over the last few days he'd accepted that he was in love with her. He'd begun to realize it at the karaoke restaurant a few days earlier, but when she'd refused to see him he'd known he had to have her in his life and that he wanted to be with her every day.

He heard footsteps approaching. A moment later the door swung open.

There she stood, looking gorgeous. She wore a flowy black skirt with a sapphire blue blouse and her blonde hair looked as pretty as ever. But the thing that struck him the most were her eyes. They really were a window to the soul, and right now her soul seemed to be in a state of mixed emotions.

"You look lovely," he said. She was studying him like she was trying to figure out what was going on in his head. He was wondering the same thing about her. "Shall we go?"

She nodded, then stepped through the door and closed it behind her.

Soon, they were seated in a quiet booth at The Glasshouse with their meals in front of them. As they ate, they talked about non-wedding things, but when they were nearly done eating, Chase finally turned the conversation to the wedding. "How did the fitting go yesterday?"

At Chase's question, Ashleigh immediately pictured herself in the wedding gown, the tiara nestled in her hair and the veil flowing down her back. The fantasy of walking down the aisle toward a man who was madly in love with her swept over her again, but she crushed it before it could bring on that familiar sadness that she'd grown used to.

"It went great," she said. "Fiona is amazing. Everything's ready. In fact, the wedding gown arrived at my house earlier today."

"Fiona came highly recommended."

Ashleigh laughed. Without his money, there was no way Fiona Cunningham would have rushed everything through the way she did. Thinking about the fitting reminded her about Jordyn's words. "Your sister is sure protective of you."

His eyebrows furrowed. "What do you mean?"

Ashleigh held back a frown. "Yesterday she told me that you've been upset." She sighed. "You're worried I won't go through with the wedding."

"I admit," Chase said with a half-smile, "that did cross my mind."

She knew it! All he cared about was the stupid wedding. He didn't care about her at all. It was so backwards and upside down. A wedding should be about the man and woman promising to love each other forever, not about pretending.

All of a sudden it was too much. She never should have agreed to the engagement, let alone a wedding. She couldn't do it, couldn't go through with it, just as she'd known would happen. She hadn't been able to trick her heart into believing it was pretend. She loved him too much.

Tears flooded her eyes. Using her cloth napkin, she wiped at them, but they wouldn't stop flowing.

"Ashleigh."

She met Chase's gaze, but fearing if she opened her mouth she would start sobbing and not be able to stop, she kept her lips clamped shut.

"Ashleigh, talk to me."

She couldn't, so she shook her head.

He stared at her for several long moments, then he set his jaw. "I'm calling off the wedding."

What?

He went on. "I've been so focused on making my mom happy that I haven't paid enough attention to what this charade is doing to you." He nodded as he spoke. "It's too much. I see that now." He smiled grimly. "I'm going to cancel it."

The shock of his pronouncement helped her get her tears under control. "But," she stammered, "it's tomorrow."

He shook his head as a soft smile curved his lips. "I don't care about that. I mean, I know my mom will be disappointed, but that's not the most important thing." His smile grew. "*You* are, Ashleigh. I care too much about you to put you through this when it's so upsetting." He sighed. "I've hurt you too much already. I won't do it again."

Overwhelmed by a kaleidoscope of emotions—love, gratitude, guilt, relief—Ashleigh didn't know what to say. Did he really care so much about her that he was putting her before his mother's dying wish?

He reached across the table and took her hand. "Are you all right?"

She felt bad that his mom would be disappointed, but the pressure was off. Relief surged through her. "Yes."

He gazed at her a moment. "Let's take a walk."

CHAPTER 46

*A*shleigh waited while Chase paid the bill, then they exited the restaurant together. Trees glowing with bright white lights lined the street. It was Christmas Eve. Last minute shoppers were buying gifts in the stores that were still open, but Ashleigh hardly noticed them. All she was aware of was Chase walking beside her, his presence making the butterflies in her belly flutter erratically. Still stunned by his decision to call off the wedding, she couldn't help but wonder what it meant for the two of them. If they were no longer getting pretend-married, would they stop seeing each other? Would this be the end?

The idea that he would step out of her life brought on a rush of melancholy.

"Let's sit down," Chase said. Ashleigh nodded, so he led

her to the bench where they sat side by side. He shifted his body so that he faced her. "I need to tell you something."

What was he going to say? That he appreciated that she'd been willing to do the fake wedding even though it hadn't worked out? See you around?

Trying to prepare herself to hear his final goodbye, she stayed silent.

"Three weeks ago, the last thing on my mind was coming to Emerald Falls to see you."

Here we go.

Wanting to just get it over with, Ashleigh held perfectly still in the hopes that the words wouldn't pierce too deeply.

"Then Jordyn told me that our mom's cancer was back." Sadness filled his eyes, but Ashleigh didn't move a muscle. "When I heard that, I came right home. Days later I went to your fundraiser."

That night seemed ages ago.

He chuckled. "First off, can I say how glad I am that a date with you was on the auction block?"

Despite herself, Ashleigh smiled.

"That day we went snowboarding..." He shook his head and looked away, then he met her eyes again. "And I came up with this crazy idea to pretend we were engaged. And *then* my mom suggests a Christmas wedding."

Here it comes.

His face became serious. "It was all going so well, until—" He swallowed several times like he was choking down his emotions.

She knew what was coming. *Until you couldn't handle it and now I'm going to have to break my mother's heart.* Guilt flowed over her in waves.

Chase's lips were pressed together, then he inhaled sharply through his nose before slowly breathing out. "Until..." His green eyes had an intensity Ashleigh had never seen before.

She didn't want to hear him say it. Ready to hold her hand up and stop him, when he took her hands in his, she stilled.

He cleared his throat, then tilted his chin down, his eyes still locked on hers. "Until I fell in love with you."

Wait. Had she heard him right? No. She couldn't have. It was her mind playing tricks on her. Her deepest wishes pretending to be true. She couldn't allow herself to feel the joy that was beginning to fill her heart. She had to crush it.

"Did you hear me?" he asked.

She stared dumbly at him.

He leaned closer. "Ashleigh, I love you."

Wait. He'd really said it? He loved her? It wasn't her mind playing tricks on her? A sunburst of joy exploded inside her. "You do?"

Shaky laughter filled the space between them as if he was relieved more than happy. "You're not going to run away, are you?"

Why would she run? "Why would I run?"

Now he looked confused. "You ran after we kissed the

other night, so I thought telling you might…I don't know… scare you off."

Laughter climbed her throat and poured out. Running away from him when he loved her? Never gonna happen, not in a million years.

He laughed too. "What's funny about that?"

This wasn't exactly how Chase had pictured this moment— him confessing his love and Ashleigh laughing. Maybe she'd gone mad. But at least she was still sitting beside him on the bench on this beautiful Christmas Eve.

"Oh, Chase, that's not why I ran."

"It's not?"

She shook her head, her smile wide and her eyes dancing. "No."

"Why then?"

Her smile dimmed. "Because I…" Her teeth sank into her lower lip like she was trying to stop the words from coming out.

"Tell me."

Sadness filled her eyes. "Because I couldn't bear it any longer."

He could see this was hard for her, but he was anxious to know what was in her heart. "Bear what any longer?"

"Loving you." Her voice was barely above a whisper and she looked down as she spoke.

Chase used his index finger to lift her chin, forcing her eyes to meet his. "What are you saying, Ashleigh?"

She lifted her chin off of his finger like she was determined to say the words that had been on her mind and in her heart. "I love you, Chase. I always have. And when we kissed..." She shook her head. "I knew I'd never gotten over you and that I never would." Tears filled her eyes. "I couldn't bear the thought of pretending to marry you and pretending to love you when in reality I *do* love you. So much."

It was a lot to take in, but Chase could feel the absolute sincerity of her words. She'd loved him for years and had never stopped. And now he knew that he loved her. It was kind of miraculous, really. Especially knowing that if he hadn't come home to be with him mom, he and Ashleigh never would have had this time together. Instead, they would be living their lives pretty much how they had been for years —alone.

Chase didn't necessarily believe in fate, but he couldn't deny that something beyond his understanding seemed to be orchestrating the events of his life. What did that mean? What was the universe trying to tell him?

Then it hit him, and he knew what he had to do.

CHAPTER 47

*A*shleigh had never felt this happy, never felt this optimistic. She loved Chase and he loved her. What could be better?

"You're going to think I'm crazy," Chase said with a crooked smile.

She laughed. "What could possibly be crazier than a fake wedding?"

That earned her a laugh. Still grinning, Chase said, "A real wedding."

"Wait." She squinted at him. "What?"

"I love you, Ashleigh."

She would never get tired of hearing that.

He smiled. "And you love me, right?"

She nodded vigorously.

"If I've learned anything these last few weeks, it's that life is tenuous and unpredictable." He paused several beats. "If we love each other, we should get married. For real."

All of a sudden Ashleigh couldn't catch her breath. Her heart beat like a drum and the blood drained from her face.

Chase's brow wrinkled as he peered at her. "Are you all right?"

She nodded. "I…I just…I'm a bit…"

He laughed. "I know, right?"

Drawing in a deep breath helped, and after a moment, she laughed. "You do come up with crazy ideas, Chase."

He tilted his chin down as he frowned. "Are you saying no?"

Now that he wanted to get married for real? Now that all of her wishes would come true? "No? Now, *that* is crazy." A smile blossomed on her lips. "Yes! I'm saying yes! I *will* marry you, Chase Matthews." She smirked. "The wedding's back on."

He laughed, loud and heartily then he tugged her against him.

Ashleigh snuggled there, reveling in the strength of his arms along with the security of knowing this was no longer pretend, and after a long, wonderful embrace, they drew away and smiled at each other.

He reached into a pocket of his jacket and pulled out a slim box. "I have something for you."

She looked from the box to his face. "What is it?"

He laughed. "You'll have to open it to find out."

Chuckling, she took it from him and opened the lid.

Tucked inside was an exquisite diamond necklace with matching earrings. Astonished, she lifted her gaze to his.

"It's to wear with your wedding gown."

"Oh." It hadn't occurred to her that he would buy her something like this, but now that the wedding was for real, it was even more special. Reverently closing the box, she smiled at him. "Thank you, Chase."

He lifted her chin and kissed her softly on the lips, sending the butterflies into a wild dance. "I love you."

Not sure if her heart could contain all of the happiness she was feeling, she concentrated on breathing evenly as she lay her head against his shoulder. "I love you too."

After several minutes of just being together, an image of Melanie filled Ashleigh's mind. She sat up and looked at Chase. "I have to tell Melanie our news."

Chase chuckled. "And I should probably tell Jordyn."

A sense of alarm swelled within her. From the things Jordyn had said, Ashleigh knew she wouldn't be happy to hear this news. Still, she couldn't expect Chase to keep it a secret from his sister. It wouldn't be right. Then again, Jordyn didn't have to know before the wedding, did she? "When will you tell her?"

"When I get home. What about you?"

It was so natural for him to share his good news with his sister that Ashleigh didn't have the heart to tell him to wait. She would just have to deal with the fallout.

"I'll tell Melanie when I get home." That was a problem in and of itself. What would her sister say? Again, she would just have to deal with the fallout. "When are your groomsmen getting to town?"

"They're already here. At the hotel. I told them I wanted to spend time with my fiancée this evening but that I'd hang out with them afterwards."

Ashleigh hadn't met his friends yet. They lived in Cupertino where he had his home. Which brought up a question. "Since we're really getting married"—the thought made her heart leap with exquisite joy— "where are we going to live afterwards?"

"Oh. Good question." He grinned. "I hadn't thought that far ahead."

She laughed. This was completely new to both of them, but oh so wonderful.

"How do you feel about moving to Cupertino?"

The thought sent a tremor of unease sliding through her. She'd lived in Emerald Falls for so long that no other place could possibly feel like home, right? "I...I don't know."

He stroked her jaw, sending a bolt of electricity zinging through her. "They have plenty of libraries in the Bay Area, you know."

It was too much to think about just then. First, agreeing to get married for real, and now talking about leaving her home. What if she refused? Would Chase leave her again? Horrified at the thought, she hedged. "I'll have to think about it."

He smiled. "Cupertino's only an hour and a half away. I

HER BILLIONAIRE EX-BOYFRIEND FAKE FIANCÉ

mean, I could set up an office here and commute there when I need to make an appearance."

Beyond touched, Ashleigh felt her heart expand with even more love than she'd had before, if that was possible. "You would do that? For me?"

Softly gazing at her, he said, "I would do anything for you, Ashleigh." Then he cupped one side of her face and leaned in.

He was going to kiss her. And this would be a kiss she could actually rejoice over. Nearly holding her breath, as his lips gently pressed against hers, she curled her arms around his neck and clung to him.

When they finally drew apart, Ashleigh was so full of love that she could hardly stand it. They sat together and talked about their future until it became too cold to be outside.

"You need to get back to your friends," Ashleigh said, "and I need to get a good night's sleep." She brushed her lips across his. "Tomorrow's our big day."

He drove her home, and when he kissed her goodnight on her front porch, all Ashleigh could think about was that the next day she would become his.

CHAPTER 48

"This is a joke," Melanie said. "Right?"

Ashleigh had waited until Melanie and Avery had come home from Gage's house and Melanie had put Avery to bed before she'd sat her down in their living room and told her the news.

"No," Ashleigh said with a stupid grin. "This is no joke. We're getting married for real."

Melanie put her hands up. "Wait. Walk me through everything that happened."

With great pleasure, Ashleigh replayed the entire evening, ending with, "I'm getting my happily ever after, Mel."

Melanie laughed, the sound ringing with cautious hope. "You seem extremely happy, I have to say."

"Oh, Mel. I'm ecstatic."

She smiled warmly. "Then I'm happy for you."

Touched that her sister was always there to support her, Ashleigh wrapped her arms around her. "Thank you."

Before going to hang out with his buddies, Chase went home to take care of two things. First, he had to find a real officiator to administer the wedding vows—and let the actor know he was no longer needed. Second, he needed to tell Jordyn his glorious news.

He knew his mom would know who to ask to officiate, but he had to play dumb to get her help. He found her lying in bed with the TV on.

"Hi, Mom. How are you?"

She muted the TV and patted the bedspread beside her. "I'm more interested in how your evening went." She smiled softly. "How are you feeling about the wedding tomorrow?"

If things hadn't changed with Ashleigh, who knew how he'd be feeling? As it was, he was extremely excited for the next day. "I'm feeling awesome. But I have a problem. I need to get someone to perform the wedding."

Her eyebrows shot up. "You mean you're getting a *real* pastor instead of a fake one?"

Wait, what? Chase's mouth opened, but nothing came out.

His mom laughed. "You thought you had me fooled, Chase, didn't you?"

He found his voice. "Did Jordyn tell you?"

Smiling, she shook her head. "No."

"How...how did you figure it out?" He'd thought they'd been so clever.

"I know you too well, son. You've never been one to jump into something so fast." Her eyes twinkled. "But I played along because I just knew there would be a Christmas miracle." Tears filled her eyes. "You love her, don't you?"

Flabbergasted, Chase could only nod.

Placing her hand on his arm, she smiled. "Okay then. Let's call Pastor Grant."

It had been a number of years since Chase had seen Pastor Grant, but he could picture him. Thin, balding, glasses, and very kind.

Ten minutes later, they had a commitment from Pastor Grant to officiate at the wedding.

After chatting with his mom for a while longer, he told her goodnight, then he went to find Jordyn.

CHAPTER 49

*C*hase woke early on Christmas morning. He had a few final arrangements to make before the wedding that he hadn't told Ashleigh about.

After enjoying a big breakfast with his mom, Jordyn, and his three groomsmen, they opened presents in front of the tree. Chase noticed that Jordyn and Brian Foster seemed to be flirting quite a bit. Since they were both single, and since Chase already knew that Brian was a great guy, this made Chase happy.

Later that afternoon, he and his groomsmen headed to the venue to get ready for his wedding.

An hour before the wedding, as Chase adjusted his tuxedo, he had to work to calm his racing heart. He was getting married that day. To Ashleigh. For real.

He waited for his feet to get cold, as it were, but it didn't happen. The only emotions he felt were happiness and excitement.

Today he would make Ashleigh his.

Today Ashleigh would become Mrs. Chase Matthews. Trying to relax as people worked on her hair and makeup, Ashleigh tried to imagine what she would feel as she and Chase were pronounced husband and wife. The feelings of delight and anticipation going through her were nearly indescribable. Ever since Sheila had suggested a Christmas Day wedding and Chase had agreed to it, she'd been dreading it. Now though, to be marrying him for real, it was her wildest dream come true.

A knock sounded at the door of the room they were using to get ready.

"Come in," she called out. Half hoping it would be Chase, when Jordyn appeared, Ashleigh felt her heart lurch. The bridesmaids had been getting ready in the room next door, so why was Jordyn there? Putting on a friendly face, Ashleigh said, "Hi, Jordyn."

She came in and closed the door behind her, her expression giving nothing away. "I need to talk to you."

Uh-oh. Ashleigh didn't want to have bad feelings between them right before she walked down the aisle. "Can it wait?"

Jordyn shook her head. "No."

Great.

Ashleigh motioned to a nearby chair.

Jordyn glanced at the women who were working on Ashleigh's hair and makeup, then smiled. "I owe you an apology."

Oh. Relieved that *that* was the direction Jordyn was going, Ashleigh felt herself relax.

"I've said some things that you may have misconstrued."

Although she wanted to ask for specifics, Ashleigh stayed silent.

"I just want you to know that I'm thrilled for you and Chase and that…well, I know you'll make him happy."

Knowing that it couldn't have been easy for Jordyn to come in there and say those things, Ashleigh smiled warmly. "I love him, Jordyn."

A soft smile curved Jordyn's lips like she'd finally figured that out. "I know you do." She stood. "I'd better finish getting ready." Her smile grew. "I'll see you in a little while."

Ashleigh nodded. "Thank you."

After Jordyn left, Ashleigh felt like everything had been set right and now she would truly be able to enjoy this special day.

Twenty minutes later, Melanie, Jordyn, and Taylor joined Ashleigh in the bride's room. Her hair and makeup were done. It was time to put on her wedding gown. Being careful not to mess up her hair or makeup, Ashleigh managed to get the gown on, then the woman who had done her hair helped her put the tiara and veil in place. Finally, Ashleigh put on the diamond necklace and earrings Chase had given her the night before.

Ashleigh looked at herself in the floor to ceiling mirror. Everything looked perfect and she knew she looked radiant. But that was only a reflection of how she felt.

"Oh, Ash," Melanie breathed as tears filled her eyes. "You look so beautiful."

"You really do," Jordyn said with a warm smile.

"This is going to be the best day ever," Taylor added.

So grateful for her sister and friends, Ashleigh felt tears pushing against her eyes. "Don't make me cry," she laughed. "It will mess up my makeup."

A knock sounded at the door. "It's time," Deena, the wedding planner said as she poked her head in. Her eyes went to Ashleigh and she smiled. "Aren't you stunning? Your groom will be..." She shook her head and chuckled. "Well, we shall see how he reacts, won't we?"

Chase, Ashleigh thought, eager to see him and to pronounce her vows to him.

Melanie, Jordyn, and Taylor each gave Ashleigh a hug, then they left the room.

Chase stood at the front of the room with Pastor Grant standing nearby. The space was small and intimate with only family and close friends there to witness this special day. A small ensemble of musicians—not the band who would be performing at the reception—played in the background. Chase's mom sat in the front row, her eyes bright. Today was the first day he'd seen her so full of energy. He knew she would be exhausted tomorrow, but he was glad she was feeling good on this wonderful day.

The tone of the music changed, which caught Chase's attention. His gaze went to the back of the room. A moment later Melanie and Josh began walking down the aisle. After them was Jordyn and Brian, then Taylor and Aaron. Finally, Avery came down the aisle carrying a basket full of red rose petals. Wearing a huge smile, she tossed the petals onto the carpet as she walked toward the front. When she reached the front, Gage motioned for her to join him in the first row, which she did.

When all of the groomsmen and bridesmaid stood arrayed around Chase, the Wedding March began. Eyes riveted to the place where Ashleigh would come through, Chase was filled with breathless anticipation.

Seconds later, she was there. She'd decided to walk herself down the aisle, and as she slowly made her way toward him, the love he had for her expanded to infinite levels and he felt tears spring into his eyes. Smiling like an idiot, he blinked rapidly to clear his tears away so he could see his beautiful bride.

This was truly the happiest day of Ashleigh's life. As she took small steps down the aisle, she barely noticed her friends watching. The only thing she could focus on was Chase and that brilliant smile. She knew it was non-traditional for her to walk herself down the aisle, but she'd wanted to do it not only because there was no one in her life who was the right person to walk her, but because it was her way of showing Chase and the world that she was doing this as an independent woman who gave herself freely to the man she loved.

For a moment, she considered what it would have been like if this had been the fake wedding they'd originally envisioned. To see Chase and to love him and to know it was all pretend would have been excruciating.

But it wasn't fake. It was real. So very, very real.

Heart filled to bursting with an unimaginable love, Ashleigh reached Chase and placed her hands in his. Pastor Grant welcomed everyone before facing Chase and Ashleigh as he talked about the commitment of marriage. Then he came to the part Ashleigh had been waiting for—the part where she and Chase exchanged vows and rings. As Chase committed himself to her, Ashleigh let her tears flow freely, and when it was her turn to let the world know how much she loved him, she did it with enthusiasm. Finally, Pastor Grant pronounced them husband and wife. She was his! Truly.

"You may kiss the bride," Pastor Grant said with a smile.

Eager for her husband's kiss, Ashleigh tilted her chin up. Chase leaned toward her and gazed into her eyes for a moment before pressing his lips against hers. Applause sounded, but Ashleigh hardly heard it, so caught up was she in his kiss. Finally, they drew apart, and with her hand clasped in his, they faced their friends and family.

Ashleigh's gaze went to Sheila, whose face was glowing with happiness. Chase had told Ashleigh how Sheila had never been fooled by their fake engagement. On impulse, Ashleigh went to her new mother-in-law and wrapped her in a gentle hug, and when Ashleigh stepped back and smiled at her, Sheila had tears in her eyes.

Chase joined her, giving his mother a hug, then he took Ashleigh's hand as they accepted congratulations from all who were there.

Melanie was one of the first to give them both hugs. "I'm so happy for you," she said to Ashleigh, her eyes bright.

"Thank you."

Then she hugged Chase. "Congratulations."

Ashleigh was pleased to see Melanie's full acceptance of Chase as her husband.

Jordyn was there next. After congratulating them both, she hugged Ashleigh, then said, "Welcome to our family."

Touched by her sincerity, Ashleigh hugged her tightly, then pulled away and smiled. "I can never have too many sisters."

After everyone had had a chance to congratulate them, Ashleigh, with her hand clasped in Chase's, led the way into an adjoining dining room where a full meal had been prepared.

The evening was more wonderful than Ashleigh could

have ever imagined. Every detail was perfect, including the beautiful cake Gage had made for them. When it was time to leave, Ashleigh changed into her going away outfit—a deep blue dress that she'd bought recently.

All the guests lined up outside to wish them farewell, but as Ashleigh held Chase's hand—she didn't know if she would ever let go—she saw something at the curb that made her stop and gasp.

She turned to Chase with a look of astonishment. "What. Is. That?"

He laughed, clearly delighted by her reaction. "Your Bookmobile."

She looked from him to the Bookmobile parked at the curb and back again. "But...I...I said I didn't want you to get one."

His smile only grew. "That just made me want to get it even more."

She wrapped her arms around him. "Oh, Chase, you are so wonderful."

He chuckled and held her tight as the crowd cheered.

She released him. "How did you even know which one to get?"

Looking toward their friends lined up, he said, "Taylor helped me pick one out."

At that, Taylor rushed over, a huge grin on her face. "Surprise!"

Not able to stop her laughter from bubbling out, Ashleigh hugged her. "How did you manage to keep this a secret?"

"It wasn't easy."

Ashleigh turned to Chase. "How did you get one delivered so fast?"

"That's where we got lucky. Someone had ordered one and had to cancel, but it was already finished." Eyebrow arching, he added, "Win-win."

Still dumbfounded, all Ashleigh could say was, "Thank you. So much."

"We'll leave it here for Taylor to manage." He lifted his chin toward another vehicle. "We're leaving in that."

Ashleigh turned to see a long, black limo parked behind the Bookmobile. Finally, they began making their way toward it. Their guests used the small bottles they'd been given to blow bubbles at Chase and Ashleigh as they walked hand in hand past them.

Chase helped Ashleigh inside, and after the chauffeur closed the door, the world quieted. It was just the two of them now, husband and wife. Laying her head against Chase's chest, Ashleigh savored this moment, and as they pulled away from the curb, she felt a peace and a calm that she hoped would last forever.

"Merry Christmas," Chase said to Ashleigh as they sat in front of their Christmas tree. Not only was it Christmas morning, but it was their first wedding anniversary. It had been the best and worst year of Chase's life. Being married to Ashleigh was better than he could have imagined, but when his mom had passed away three weeks after the wedding, it had been devastating. He was just grateful Ashleigh had been by his side to help him get through it.

"Merry Christmas to you," Ashleigh said with a smile, then she handed him a small box. "For you."

He shook the box. It made a rattling sound. Intrigued, he took off the festive wrapping paper, then opened the box. Inside was a tiny green baby rattle. Knowing what it meant, but still shocked, he looked at Ashleigh with raised eyebrows. "Does this mean…?" He let his words trail off.

He didn't know if he'd ever seen her smile so bright. "Yes. We're having a baby."

They'd talked about starting a family but hadn't been sure when the right time was. Looked like the decision was out of their hands.

Supremely pleased, Chase pulled Ashleigh onto his lap and nuzzled her neck. "I hope it's a girl who looks just like you."

She laughed. "If it's a girl, she'll have you wrapped around her finger in no time."

Laughing happily, Chase nodded. "True."

Ashleigh hadn't been sure how Chase would react to her news. But seeing his pure delight, she didn't know why she'd worried—he was so good to her. How many times had he done things to surprise her, just to show her that he was thinking about her? He was wonderful.

"Guess we'll need to get a nursery ready," he said with a grin.

After their honeymoon, they'd bought a large house in Emerald Falls—Ashleigh had told Melanie that she and Avery could stay in her house as long as they wanted, although Melanie and Gage had recently gotten engaged so she would be moving out eventually.

"Yes," Ashleigh said with new excitement as she began picturing how she wanted to decorate. Life was good. She still worked as the Emerald Falls librarian, and the Bookmobile had been a big hit.

The last year had been filled with great joy and extreme sadness, but the bond Ashleigh had with Chase was stronger than ever. Though their relationship had started off to make someone else happy, in the end it was Chase and Ashleigh who had found their happily ever after.

ABOUT THE AUTHOR

Christine has always loved to read, but enjoys writing suspenseful novels as well. She has her own eReader and is not embarrassed to admit that she is a book hoarder. One of Christine's favorite activities is to go camping with her family and read, read, read while enjoying the beauty of nature.

I love to hear from my readers. You can contact me in any of the following ways:
www.christinekersey.com
christine@christinekersey.com

Made in the USA
Las Vegas, NV
19 March 2021

19833510R00177